"NO ONE HAS EVER HAD THE NERVE TO TELL ME OFF THE WAY YOU JUST DID."

"Perhaps if they did, you wouldn't be the rampant egotist you are today."

Jared blinked at this bit of biting honesty. He'd never come across a woman who refused to succumb to his charms. The thought of Alex's immunity rankled.

"The navy certainly added iron to your backbone," he said, speaking softly. "But I wonder if the rest of you is cast in iron as well."

Alex was totally unprepared for Jared as he pulled her into his arms and his mouth descended on hers. Disjointed thoughts ran through her brain, gauging her own reactions to this unexpected attack. Her traitorous body had already melted against Jared's hard form while her arms slowly lifted to circle his neck.

A CANDLELIGHT ECSTASY ROMANCE ®

154 A SEASON FOR LOVE, *Heather Graham*
155 LOVING ADVERSARIES, *Eileen Bryan*
156 KISS THE TEARS AWAY, *Anna Hudson*
157 WILDFIRE, *Cathie Linz*
158 DESIRE AND CONQUER, *Diane Dunaway*
159 A FLIGHT OF SPLENDOR, *Joellyn Carroll*
160 FOOL'S PARADISE, *Linda Vail*
161 A DANGEROUS HAVEN, *Shirley Hart*
162 VIDEO VIXEN, *Elaine Raco Chase*
163 BRIAN'S CAPTIVE, *Alexis Hill Jordan*
164 ILLUSIVE LOVER, *Jo Calloway*
165 A PASSIONATE VENTURE, *Julia Howard*
166 NO PROMISE GIVEN, *Donna Kimel Vitek*
167 BENEATH THE WILLOW TREE, *Emma Bennett*
168 CHAMPAGNE FLIGHT, *Prudence Martin*
169 INTERLUDE OF LOVE, *Beverly Sommers*
170 PROMISES IN THE NIGHT, *Jackie Black*
171 HOLD LOVE TIGHTLY, *Megan Lane*
172 ENDURING LOVE, *Tate McKenna*
173 RESTLESS WIND, *Margaret Dobson*
174 TEMPESTUOUS CHALLENGE, *Eleanor Woods*
175 TENDER TORMENT, *Harper McBride*
176 PASSIONATE DECEIVER, *Barbara Andrews*
177 QUIET WALKS THE TIGER, *Heather Graham*
178 A SUMMER'S EMBRACE, *Cathie Linz*
179 DESERT SPLENDOR, *Samantha Hughes*
180 LOST WITHOUT LOVE, *Elizabeth Raffel*
181 A TEMPTING STRANGER, *Lori Copeland*
182 DELICATE BALANCE, *Emily Elliott*
183 A NIGHT TO REMEMBER, *Shirley Hart*
184 DARK SURRENDER, *Diana Blayne*
185 TURN BACK THE DAWN, *Nell Kincaid*
186 GEMSTONE, *Bonnie Drake*
187 A TIME TO LOVE, *Jackie Black*
188 WINDSONG, *Jo Calloway*
189 LOVE'S MADNESS, *Sheila Paulos*
190 DESTINY'S TOUCH, *Dorothy Ann Bernard*
191 NO OTHER LOVE, *Alyssa Morgan*
192 THE DEDICATED MAN, *Lass Small*
193 MEMORY AND DESIRE, *Eileen Bryan*

GUARDIAN ANGEL

Linda Randall Wisdom

A CANDLELIGHT ECSTASY ROMANCE ®

Published by
Dell Publishing Co., Inc.
1 Dag Hammarskjold Plaza
New York, New York 10017

ISBN: 0-440-13274-6

Printed in the United States of America
First printing—December 1983

To Our Readers:

We have been delighted with your enthusiastic response to Candlelight Ecstasy Romances®, and we thank you for the interest you have shown in this exciting series.

In the upcoming months we will continue to present the distinctive sensuous love stories you have come to expect only from Ecstasy. We look forward to bringing you many more books from your favorite authors and also the very finest work from new authors of contemporary romantic fiction.

As always, we are striving to present the unique, absorbing love stories that you enjoy most—books that are more than ordinary romance.

Your suggestions and comments are always welcome. Please write to us at the address below.

Sincerely,

The Editors
Candlelight Romances
1 Dag Hammarskjold Plaza
New York, New York 10017

GUARDIAN ANGEL

CHAPTER ONE

The high tiled dome that housed the olympic-size swimming pool was quiet except for its lone occupant. Sounds of a body moving through water echoed in the cavernous room; pool lights, the only illumination, warmly caressed the swimmer.

The body was male and used to strenuous exercise. He easily navigated laps, touching the side, completing a flip turn, and striking out again. Each stroke was smooth and practiced. A few minutes later his strong hands gripped the edge and his well-toned arms strained to propel him out of the water.

He picked up a large white towel from a lounge chair, and patted his flat stomach dry, moving the towel upward to his broad chest lightly covered with dark hair, then down to his long legs, also covered with crisp, curling hair. His grass-green eyes didn't look up when the sound of footsteps rang on the tiled floor. He didn't need to turn around to identify his visitor.

She was tall—five feet eight inches according to the personnel records—her extremely slender body dressed in a navy skirt and jacket and white crepe de chine blouse. Shoulder-length dark brown hair was brushed up into a smooth coil on top of her head, emphasizing her delicate throat and her large mint-green eyes.

"They're assembled in the executive conference room, Mr. Templeton." Her husky, sensual voice carried easily across the room.

Jared Templeton slowly turned and nonchalantly draped his towel around his shoulders. He stood in a relaxed pose that was far from casual as far as the woman was concerned. She was well aware he was wearing the briefest of swimming suits in a dark navy that may have covered his masculinity, but it certainly didn't hide it!

"And eagerly awaiting my presence, I'm sure," he commented in a dry voice, raking his fingers through wet hair and flicking it away from his face. "I'll be sure not to disappoint them. Tell Chris I'll be there in twenty minutes. It won't hurt the press to wait a little longer for their story."

The woman inclined her head and walked out, her footsteps fading in the distance. Jared didn't bother to leave just yet. There were no doubts in his mind that she wouldn't carry out his instructions.

The woman took the elevator down two floors, where it opened out onto a plush reception area guarding the executive suites. She smiled briefly at the receptionist seated behind an antique French desk and entered one of the doors set off to one side.

The man seated behind the desk had been chosen all-American in college and ten years later still kept his muscular physique in excellent shape. He lifted a questioning eyebrow as the woman dropped into the chair across from him.

"Let's see," she frowned thoughtfully, her fingertips

touching each other in the form of a steeple, "shall I make reservations at Ma Maison or perhaps . . ."

"Not again!" he groaned, his face screwed up in a pained grimace. He leaned back in his chair, hands covering his eyes. "Are you sure the two of you aren't conspiring to break me? At this rate you're going to be a very pudgy lady and at your age you can't afford that, you know," he teased with mischief dancing in his eyes.

She winced at his none too subtle reminder that her so-called carefree twenties were a thing of the past. "Chris, you have a sadistic streak in you," she accused him with a good-natured air. "Actually, he said he'd be down in twenty minutes."

Chris glanced at the clock and stood up, one hand raised to straighten his tie. "Well, milady, shall we face the mob?"

The huge conference room, used for meetings such as today's, was filled to capacity with members of the press and television reporters. Videotape cameras from every television news show were eagerly jostling for the best place to film one of the great businessmen of the decade. Talk was loud and chaotic until a side door opened and three people walked toward the podium ringed with microphones.

The man they were anxious to hear was flanked by the muscular Chris on one side and the dark-haired woman, her patrician features composed into a cool mask, on the other.

"Alex Page," one writer for a well-known financial trade magazine muttered to the man seated next to him.

"Which one?"

"The one with the great-looking legs. Her full name is Alexis." He grinned while his eyes assessed the tall, slender woman. "She's Templeton's bodyguard."

"What?" The other man was clearly surprised by this piece of information.

"That's what they call her anyway." He shook his head, not really believing that a good-looking woman could be hired to guard a man. "She began working for him six months ago as his Chief of Security and travels with him constantly. Rumor has it that she's his mistress, but the social columns have reported him out with just about every socialite in the world. He plays the field like you wouldn't believe. Very little is given out on Alex Page, only that she's a graduate of Annapolis and worked in Naval Intelligence before she resigned her commission. For such a young woman, she's done quite a bit with her life. Her father is *the* Admiral Hayden who's been making all those waves in the Pentagon."

The other man now watched Alex with awe. How could someone so lovely be in such an intimidating position?

The female portion of the audience watched Jared with hungry eyes. Alex stood off to one side and watched them with an amused glint in her eyes. These women were devouring him the way a wolf goes after its prey. She silently wondered what the reaction would have been if any of them had seen Jared earlier while he had been swimming. She decided that the show would have been immensely enjoyed by all. She preferred to forget what Jared's camel-colored three-piece suit, bronze silk shirt, and striped tie of gold and brown hid from the audience, but even these trappings of civilization couldn't hide the barely leashed power of the man. His toffee-colored hair was brushed away from his face, with only the wings of gray at the temples attesting to his forty years. Even the slight hump on the bridge of his nose couldn't detract from his male attractiveness.

"Ladies and gentlemen." His voice rang out rich and deep. There would be no apology for his tardiness. None was needed. A small smile with a hint of sensuality curved his lips as he looked at the group calmly awaiting his words. "Now that you've enjoyed our pastries and coffee, it's time to work for them." His eyes fell briefly on each woman, making her feel as if he were speaking to her individually. "I'll take pity on you and be brief. This morning at nine o'clock, Fernwood Enterprises signed the contract to buy the Manning Refinery." He paused, allowing the hum of conversation to die down.

"No more depending on other people, Mr. Templeton?" one man called out.

"You know as well as I do, Sam, that if you don't do your own work, it never gets done," Jared replied. "Printed statements will be made available to you, giving all the statistics, and I'll give you twenty minutes for questions."

"Sometimes I wonder why he bothers having us here," Chris muttered to Alex as the questions flew fast and furious to Jared. "We just sit back here and twiddle our thumbs."

"We both know why I'm here." She hadn't taken her eyes off the members of the press once.

"Mr. Templeton, is it true you're still receiving threats on your life?" one man spoke up.

"I'm in a touchy profession. I doubt I'm the only person to receive threats of any nature. Whether they're cranks or not is something else. I believe in taking the necessary precautions, just in case," he replied.

All eyes swiveled to the side where Alex stood.

"Couldn't that be hard on your social life?" one blond woman asked archly.

Jared's husky laugh sent shivers down the women's spines. "Perhaps the ladies I escort are the ones I need protection from," he answered, creating laughter throughout the room.

After the time allotted for questions was over, the trio left. The women watched Jared's leavetaking with dreams in their eyes while the men studied Alex with a different kind of hunger.

"That kind of lady could guard me around the clock," one man muttered while he packed up his camera equipment.

A private elevator whisked Jared, Alex, and Chris to the executive floor while Jared rapidly issued instructions to Chris.

"See if my appointments can be canceled for tomorrow so we can fly out first thing in the morning to check on those new office condos going up. Then call Warner and ask if those contracts for the deal with Donaldson are drawn up yet. If they aren't, tell him I want them by the following day." The elevator doors silently slid open and Jared was still talking as he strode down the hall to a pair of ornate carved-oak doors. These led to the office of the president and chairman of the board to Fernwood Enterprises, Jared D. Templeton.

Chris walked off through one of the doors that led to his office and picked up the telephone message slips for Jared. He would prescreen them before any were seen by his boss.

Alex cocked a questioning eyebrow at Jared. Receiving his nod, she slipped off her jacket. A narrow, dark brown leather strap circled her shoulders with a small holster cradled just under her right armpit.

Jared grimaced as he watched her slip off the harness and lay it on the couch. "After watching you handle that thing on the practice range that one day, I know I sure wouldn't want to get in your way." He opened a small polished wooden box and withdrew a cheroot.

"That's why you hired me." She looked up when the

receptionist knocked and stuck her head in the door to inquire if anyone wanted coffee; both declined.

His eyes narrowed from the spiraling smoke of his cheroot, Jared sat back in his chair and watched Alex cross the room. He couldn't remember ever meeting a more striking woman. She couldn't be called beautiful—her face and body were too slender for that—but she carried herself with the grace of a greyhound. The lines of a Thoroughbred, his grandmother would say, but much too small in the hips.

"Does it bother you that many people refuse to believe you're my bodyguard?" His lazy voice easily carried across the room.

Alex was amused by his question and not completely surprised. Jared enjoyed injecting these little intimate nuances every chance he got. Now she merely ignored them. "I never think about it," she replied honestly.

Jared's fingers drummed on the polished wood desk. It had become a game with him to see how far he could push her before her composure would crack. So far he hadn't won. "You have to admit that it's difficult to believe such a lovely lady would have such a dangerous job."

"No more than when I worked in Naval Intelligence." She shrugged, a little surprised by Jared's remarks about her looks. He had escorted all too many beautiful women in the past to think that she was lovely. At the same time, an inner sense had told her from the beginning that Jared was more than interested in her. She knew that she presented a challenge to him since she didn't hang on to his every word the way his other women had; yet, if she had, there wouldn't be any challenge! Alex had no need for a man in her life just now and Jared Templeton certainly wouldn't be the one to fill it if she did. Granted, he was attractive and always mindful of a woman's needs, but she didn't care to be part of a package plan. She didn't want to get into any personal discussions with him and had succeeded this long. "If you don't need me any longer, I'll go down to my office."

Jared nodded. He was already immersed in the papers on his desk, the playboy part of him covered by the astute businessman.

Chris detained Alex as she left the office. "Okay, you won the bet. The chief kept the press waiting this time and I now owe you a meal . . . again." He heaved a mock sigh. "How is it you can read his mind better than his personal assistant? That's not fair, Alex! Are you sure he isn't on your side in breaking my bankroll?"

"Don't expect any pity from me, Chris Stevens." She wasn't moved by his act. "As for reading minds, let's just say I've always been blessed with ESP. I'll see you later."

"How did the press conference go?" Dena, Alex's secretary, greeted her when she stopped at her desk for messages.

"The usual." She shrugged as she sifted through her message slips. "Did Mr. Ford call with the estimates for those new cameras for the parking garage?"

"Not yet. Do you want me to get in touch with him?"

She shook her head as she glanced down at her watch. "No, it can wait. At least it will have to because I have to fly out with Mr. Templeton tomorrow morning."

"Anyone who didn't know better would envy you your travels," her secretary told her. "Chris already called me with the details. You'll be picked up at your apartment at six A.M."

Alex grimaced. "Sometimes I wonder why I bother having an office or a home. I never seem to spend very much time in either. Why don't you go home now. I'm going to stay and catch up on my paperwork and leave some dictation for you. There's also no reason why you can't make it an early day tomorrow."

"Um, I knew there was a reason why I enjoy working for you." Dena's eyes sparkled. "Even if you are a slave-driver," she teased.

"You got it." Alex's laughter was husky. "Have a good evening, Dena. I'll see you day after tomorrow."

She always felt her office was one of the few places she could relax in. She had been allowed to decorate it anyway she wished and had furnished it with antiques. She was especially fond of her prized possession, a highly polished oak rolltop desk. A comfortable-looking dark blue sofa sat against one wall along with an old-fashioned wooden table. Instead of carpeting, a deep burgundy rug covered the floor. Even the file cabinet was an antique. A large bookcase with glass doors stood near the window.

Alex glanced out the window to the narrow strip far below that was, in reality, a busy main boulevard in Century City. She was tired, more tired than she cared to admit. She sat down in her deeply cushioned chair and rested her head against the back. She closed her eyes for a few blessed moments. The day before, she and Jared, along with Chris, had returned from a three-day trip to Alaska and she still hadn't had a chance to catch up on her rest.

"I'm getting too old for this." She gave a short laugh, then turned back to her paperwork.

As usual, when Alex worked, she lost track of time. When Jared first hired her he had made it clear that she was to be on call to travel with him at all times. He had wanted a bodyguard, nothing more. At the same time, Alex stressed the point that she wouldn't sit around doing nothing when she wasn't needed. Hence, she was groomed to take over as Chief of Security when John Lyons, the previous chief, had retired four months ago. She had been lucky that he was an open-minded man who appreciated her value as an expert in security devices. John had taught her a great many of his own secrets before his retirement and enjoyed meeting Alex for lunch whenever she had a free day.

Lately Alex had been working to set up a tighter security system in the employee parking garage. She had read enough newspaper stories about women being assaulted when they left work to know she had to do whatever was possible to insure it wouldn't happen here.

It wasn't until after nine that Alex finally descended in the elevator and signed herself out with a brief smile to the security guard stationed near the entrance.

"Have a good evening, Mrs. Page," the man told her as he let her out the front door.

Alex was able to grab a cab at the nearby taxi stand and gave the driver her address. All she wanted now was a hot shower and bed.

Needing an easy access to the downtown Los Angeles area, she had chosen to live in Marina del Rey, where the many apartment buildings and condominium complexes reminded her of a rabbit warren. But she didn't spend much time at home, so it didn't matter.

When she reached her apartment she slipped off her shoes and carried them into the bedroom. Habits carried over from growing up in a military family and being in the service herself decreed that everything have its place.

After a hot shower Alex dismissed the idea of a late dinner and fixed herself a cup of tea instead.

There were few personal items scattered about the spacious one-bedroom apartment, the most prominent being photographs of her family. All the men were in naval uniforms and there was one of Alex in her dress whites, a set of lieutenant bars gleaming on her shoulders. How long ago that was!

Alex scribbled a note for the cleaning woman who came in twice a week, then decided bed was the best place for her if she had to be ready early the next morning. Jared's driver would pick her up for the short trip to the airport. There had been so many of these trips this past month, yet it didn't even bother her. Not even the lack of a social life seemed depressing. She considered herself too busy with her work to think that she actually led quite a lonely life.

"Damn!" she muttered the next morning when she discovered she was out of coffee. "Now I'll have to wait until I board the jet," she grumbled, slamming the cabinet door shut and making a note to pick up coffee when she did her grocery shopping that weekend.

Her gun and holster were taken out of its locked drawer and slipped over her crimson blouse and under a black wool jacket. "No wonder I feel like a gangster." She laughed to herself, picking up the oxblood-colored leather briefcase that doubled as a purse.

Promptly at six Alex stepped into a black limousine waiting outside her apartment building.

"Another early morning for us, Frank," she told the stocky, gray-haired man. "Tell me, does Mr. Templeton ever give you a chance to sleep?"

The driver replied with a laugh. "I could ask the same of you, Mrs. Page. Except for Mr. Templeton, you're usually the first one in and the last one out of the office." He respected this quiet woman who never kept him waiting and never patronized him the way Mr. Templeton's lady friends had a habit of doing.

"I'm surprised you didn't pick Mr. Templeton up first," she commented, settling back against the plush seat.

"He's already at the airport, I expect. Said he'd be having a late night and would drive himself in."

Alex's green eyes sparkled with suppressed humor. A

late night meant a woman and Jared certainly had his pick of those!

Frank drove to the part of the airport that housed the private planes. After being passed into the hanger area, the limousine sped toward a waiting white and gold Learjet.

Alex hurriedly boarded the jet and found Jared and Chris already aboard. Jared glanced up before returning to the papers in his hand.

"Chris, would you let Cal know we're ready to leave now?"

Alex took her usual seat near one of the windows and buckled her seat belt. After following Jared's instructions, Chris dropped into the seat beside her.

"I found a great hamburger joint downtown and I thought we could try it tomorrow for lunch," he suggested casually.

Alex shook her head. "No way, I'm having Dena make reservations at the most expensive restaurant this state has to offer," she teased.

"You're heartless."

"Chris, these figures need to be verified." Jared abruptly interrupted their conversation.

"Sure, boss." As soon as the jet had lifted into the air, Chris hauled himself out of his seat. "There's coffee brewing. Since you're not too amiable this morning, you must not have had your morning ration of caffeine yet," he told Alex.

"Ration? I didn't even have enough coffee to make one cup." She also rose to walk over to the bar where a coffee urn sat, unaware that Jared's hooded gaze followed her progress. She poured herself a cup, then turned to catch Jared's eyes on her. "Would you care for a cup of coffee, Mr. Templeton?" she asked politely.

At his affirmative nod, Alex set her cup aside, poured another, and added two sugars. She wondered, with bemusement, if his mistresses knew his tastes as well as she and Chris did, then corrected herself. Naturally they would know how he took his coffee and even more personal tastes that she and Chris had nothing to do with.

"What a pity you can't type, Alex," Jared murmured when he accepted the steaming cup. "Then I wouldn't need Chris."

"I'm lucky that Naval Intelligence didn't believe in typing skills then, aren't I?" she countered, walking back over to pick up her own cup and return to her seat. "I do so much better at tracking down the lower elements." She presented him with a dazzling smile.

"She's talking about me again, boss," Chris said.

Amused glints appeared in Jared's eyes that speared and held Alex's gaze. "No, I believe the lady is referring to me this time."

When they reached the Seattle airport, Chris looked out at the rain pouring down in sheets.

"Why does it rain every time we fly in here?" he complained, gathering file folders and pushing them into his briefcase.

"Probably because you hate wet weather so much." Alex retrieved her raincoat from a closet that held changes of clothing for all of them for these type of emergencies. There had also been times when she had slept in the adjoining bedroom when they were on longer flights.

A limousine waited for them on one of the ramps and Theodore Saunders, in charge of the Seattle operations, greeted Jared with a smile and handshake. It wasn't long before they were transported to one of the more affluent business sections of the city. Mr. Saunders eyed Alex and Chris curiously as he had the other two times they had accompanied Jared to Seattle. It had been hard for him to assimilate the idea that Alex was the bodyguard and Chris the personal assistant, or glorified secretary.

"Has the architect walked over the site yet?" Jared examined the flow of water in the streets from the heavy rainfall. "I want all the soil sample reports on my desk by the beginning of next week," he commanded as Mr. Saunders nodded.

They had lunch in a quiet restaurant before returning to the airport and ultimately, Los Angeles.

Once on board the jet, Jared excused himself to make a private telephone call.

"The Miami Missile," Chris said sotto voce when he and Alex had been left alone.

She looked surprised. "This one has lasted quite a long time."

"I think she's on her way out. He ordered the usual diamond necklace to be sent to her."

Alex laughed softly. "To make room for the Sydney Sorceress, I'm sure." She referred to the Australian cattle heiress whom Jared had escorted to several charity functions recently. The nicknames had begun as a game between Alex and Chris almost from the beginning of their working relationship. Jared was known for the beautiful women at his side and who probably shared his bed. "Whatever happened to the South Seas Siren?" she asked, referring to the woman who had been relentless in her pursuit of Jared for the past few months.

Chris's lips twitched. "She neglected to mention she had a husband."

"Really?"

"Yep, in his sixties and suffers from gout. As soon as the boss found out he let her know in no uncertain terms what he thought of unfaithful wives. She beat it back home when hubby threatened to cut off her allowance." He got up and poured two cups of coffee, handing one to Alex. "How come there's no L.A. Lover Boy in your life? Of course, you do know I have to meet him first and pass my seal of approval."

Alex inwardly flinched as the memory of her father ruthlessly inspecting every young man she dated flickered through her mind. "My schedule doesn't allow for extracurricular activities." She stifled a yawn.

"Perhaps we should rearrange your hours to give you more freedom then."

She didn't blink an eyelash at Jared's note of censure when he had walked back into the room. "I don't need any special compensations, Mr. Templeton," she drawled. "If you can manage a full social calendar, I'm sure I could, too, if I wished to do so."

Again Jared privately wondered about Alex's ex-husband. What kind of man turned her into this mechanical replica of a lovely woman?

Alex watched him cross the interior. There were times when she felt as if he were flaunting his virile masculinity at her. He was good looking, although not handsome in the conventional way. He was a man who grew more attractive with each year and she admitted that he fascinated her as a man, but that was as far as she'd go. Admitting too much could prove dangerous to her peace of mind.

"Yes, but can he cook?" she murmured under her breath, watching the way Jared's dark gray slacks hugged his lean hips and the cream silk shirt outlined his shoulders. He had discarded his jacket when they had boarded the jet and his vest was left unbuttoned. His gray and blue striped tie was loosened from his shirt collar for comfort's sake. For one crazy moment Alex wondered what he would be like as a lover. The women he had been photographed with certainly looked satisfied, if not more.

When the powerful jet touched down at Los Angeles Airport, Alex experienced an inner sigh of relief. She just might be able to make it an early night and catch up on her sleep. It had been weeks since she had tumbled into bed before midnight.

"I'll see Mrs. Page home, Frank," Jared informed the driver.

Alex turned her head around. In all the time she had worked for Jared, he had never offered to drive her home. That duty had always been left to Frank. Since Jared didn't live anywhere in the vicinity of her apartment, she couldn't understand why his offer came up today. A faint look of surprise flickered in Chris's eyes at Jared's announcement.

"Chris, move that ten o'clock meeting up to nine," Jared commanded, as he cupped his hand under Alex's elbow and guided her toward the parking lot.

Alex experienced a tingling sensation along the nerve endings in her arm where Jared's hand warmed her skin.

"You don't need to go out of your way when Frank is here to drive me." She presented a mild argument while she stood next to Jared's low-slung silver Maserati. No one protested vehemently with him, not if they wanted to survive.

He didn't answer until they were both seated in the luxurious interior of the car. "Who said that I'm going out of my way?" he asked facetiously.

Her dry answer was without hesitation. "Because I can't see any of your lady friends living in Marina del Rey. I'm sure they're much happier in Beverly Hills or Bel-Air."

The engine purred as it slowly moved toward the exit and merged with the heavy early evening traffic.

"Do you and Chris date on a regular basis?"

Alex blinked at the abrupt question. "Does betting dinners count?" she couldn't resist asking.

Jared shot her an emerald speared glance. "Would you

care to elaborate on that?" There was a grating sound in the depths of his throat.

"Hmm?" She rolled her neck around to relieve the sore muscles. Since her eyes were closed, she hadn't seen his hands tighten on the steering wheel for a brief second.

"Betting dinners," he reminded on a harsher note.

"I usually win," Alex murmured, recalling Chris's sorrow over her recent restaurant choice. She still remembered the last time he had won and the exorbitant dinner bill she had paid. Chris had taken her to the proverbial cleaners that evening.

"I'd be fascinated to know how you win all these dinners." Jared's foot tapped the brake when the traffic signal changed to red.

"We bet on your whims."

His head turned. "What?"

Alex's throaty chuckle danced in the air. "Example, when you had your press conference yesterday, Chris bet you wouldn't keep them waiting; I said you would. You did and he owes me one dinner at a restaurant of my choice."

A faint smile tugged at the corners of his mouth. "Give me another example." His silky drawl could be dangerous at times.

Alex pursed her lips in brief thought. "The time Sara mislaid your contracts for Matson?" At his nod she continued, only pausing as the light turned green and the car moved slowly forward. "Chris was positive you'd frighten her with a display of your infamous temper. I said you'd scare her even more by reacting in a calmer manner. You did and we had lunch at Nico's courtesy of Chris."

"You seem to be pretty confident of my moods," he commented.

Alex shook her head. "Not *yours,*" she corrected him softly. "Just the type of man you are."

"And what type of man am I?" Jared asked curiously.

She glanced toward the signs posted at the freeway ramp, ignoring his question. "Wait a minute, this isn't the way to my apartment." She was instantly wary.

"I thought we'd have dinner first," he continued in his silky voice, arrogantly assuming she'd agree.

"Didn't you take it into account that I might have previous plans?"

"Now, now, don't get testy," he chided. "Just think of it as my taking Chris's place. After all, you're due this dinner thanks to me."

Alex still felt a little wary about Jared's so-called kindly motive in taking her out to dinner when he hadn't done anything of this sort before. She had a sneaking suspicion that if he preferred, this wouldn't be a run-of-the-mill business dinner.

"Oh, come now, Alex, after all this time you should know you can trust me," he said humorously. "After all, you could merely use a judo hold on me if I got too close to you."

This playful banter with Jared was new to her. Their working relationship had always been kept on an impersonal basis, and now Jared was suddenly delving into her personal life by taking her out, although this couldn't be called a date. During the six months she had been working for him, she had developed a sensitive antenna where he was concerned and right now those invisible fibers were vibrating like mad.

Jared was openly studying Alex's slender curves and obviously liked what he saw. The light in his emerald eyes told her that. Alex was hoping this could be considered temporary insanity on Jared's part, and she might as well sit back and enjoy her evening.

The maître d' had seen them to their table and handed them menus before leaving.

Alex glanced around the large dining room with some surprise.

"You look puzzled," Jared commented, reaching across the table to cover her hand with his.

She turned back to him, feeling the warmth course from his hand to hers, wishing it wasn't affecting her pulse rate. "Ordinarily I wouldn't see this place as one of your haunts, yet you know the headwaiter by name and you even greeted several of the waiters by name."

"What do you see as my usual 'haunt' for dining out?" He took a cheroot out and lit it.

"Either small, candlelit, and very intimate or brightly lit and on the border of ostentatious; a place where all the right people frequent. Where a lady wouldn't be allowed to enter unless she was wearing the required number of diamonds." She looked around the well-lit restaurant interior with its homey atmosphere, then turned back to him, carefully withdrawing her hand to pick up her water glass.

Jared drew on his cheroot and silently considered Alex's words. "I guess I'm going to have to correct that impression," he mused.

"Your private life is your own business, Mr. Templeton. I merely try to insure your safety." She skillfully erected an invisible barrier.

Jared's facial muscles briefly tightened. "You're off-duty now, Alex. I can't imagine anyone would have the nerve to attack me in such a public place. Why don't you just sit back and relax. This should give us a chance to get to know each other better."

"I didn't realize my personnel file was so sketchy," she murmured in a dry voice.

His reply was interrupted by the arrival of the cocktail waitress. She bestowed a warm smile on Jared as she took their orders for Scotch and water.

"You don't like to give out any information about yourself, do you?" Jared remarked once they had been left alone again.

"Don't feel offended, Mr. Templeton." Alex's slow smile taunted his obvious displeasure at her evasive answers. "It's a common trait among ex-cops."

"Then I'm surprised you didn't stay in the navy."

Her eyes clouded over momentarily, then cleared just as quickly. "I had my reasons for resigning my commission."

"A reason no one will ever find out?" he prodded.

Alex's smile held no promises. "Would you recommend the scallops?" She picked up her menu. "I'm in the mood for seafood, I think."

He shook his head. Although she effectively closed the subject, he was equally determined to reopen it at a later date.

Alex found Jared to be an entertaining dinner companion. Over brandy and coffee they exchanged college experiences, the closest she had ever come to revealing parts of her private life.

"What prompted you to enter the Naval Academy?" Jared asked her.

Alex's fingertips idly circled the rim of her brandy snifter. "Family tradition. It was part of our upbringing." Her lips curved wryly. "My father was ecstatic when I entered the Academy."

"And his reaction when you resigned?"

She slowly raised her head. "The jury's still out."

Jared leaned back in his chair and studied her through narrowed eyes. He may have looked the urbane man totally at ease with himself, but Alex knew better. She strongly suspected that his instincts and reflexes were as finely honed as her own. A man like Jared Templeton didn't reach the position he held today without fighting every step of the way.

He was growing more curious about Alex every day he spent in her company. What were the real reasons behind her leaving the navy? What had happened with her marriage, and what was her ex-husband like? Studying the too thin angles of her face, he wondered how someone who could project such a strong sense of sensual femininity could work in a potentially dangerous job. He was well aware that the day could come when she would be forced to use the handgun she carried. A day he didn't want to think about. The written and tape-recorded threats on his life from a left-wing terrorist group regarding his oil dealings with the Middle East sheikhs had been all too explicit. He marveled at the calm exterior Alex exuded when she went over the new threats. She merely tightened the security in the building, had a new alarm system set up in his home, and was by his side at all public functions. She seemed to have a sixth sense when it came to danger, and he knew he would trust her with his life. At the same time, he still couldn't forget his unanswered questions about Alex the woman. His years at the top of the corporate ladder and dealing with multifaceted personalities told him that no amount of questioning would yield him the answers that would reveal the real Alex. Of course, that didn't mean he'd give up, merely that he'd have to redouble his efforts.

CHAPTER TWO

Alex was given a few days of peace and quiet when Jared decided to fly up to his ranch in the Santa Ynez Valley.

She had found it difficult to forget her evening out with him even though he acted correctly toward her the entire time. When he escorted her to her apartment door, he made no effort to invite himself in; instead he left after wishing her a good night.

The next afternoon Jared announced his intention to fly up to his ranch for a few days and wouldn't need Alex's services for that time.

"Here's the monthly report from the New York and Boston offices," Dena announced, entering Alex's office and laying two paperbound notebooks on her desk.

"Two days late, as usual," she commented in a dry voice. She picked up her dark-rimmed glasses and perched them on her nose. "I wonder what threats would suffice to get these here on time next month."

"You're certainly a grouch when Mr. Templeton isn't around."

Alex's eyes flew upward at this absurd idea. "I beg your pardon?"

Dena's grin was just a shade too impish. Alex's cold tone of voice intimidated other people, but the petite secretary knew her boss's bark was definitely worse than her bite. "Come on, Alex, 'fess up. All of us have some type of crush on Mr. Templeton. Don't you feel the least bit fascinated by him?"

"I don't care to be part of a crowd." She leafed through one of the reports and briefly scanned the contents. "Did you finish typing my report regarding the new security measures in the parking garage?"

Dena nodded. "As soon as I could decipher that atrocious scrawl you call handwriting. You should have been a doctor, with that kind of penmanship."

Alex grimaced, thinking of the meeting ahead of her. When it came to security measures, she didn't believe in looking at the dollars and cents of the project, only the safety it would afford, but she had soon found out that the accounting department at Fernwood very definitely looked at the cost and, more often than not, worked very hard to cut her budgets. Today would be another battle and she intended to go in there and win.

"I'm going to need every bit of ammunition I can get when I go into that meeting this afternoon. Mr. St. Clair can't seem to get it into his head that more and more assaults are happening to women in office-building parking lots. Three women were attacked in the Kovack Corporation's parking lot last month and they still haven't found the man."

Dena shuddered at the memory of reading the accounts in the newspaper. "Most of the women here are making sure they go out in groups and even park their cars in the same area. Your defense class is a big help too."

"Thanks," Alex said sincerely. "You know how much

trouble I had getting permission to use the gym after hours since they even count the extra hours of electricity used."

"Why don't you tell Mr. Templeton the problems you've been having with Mr. St. Clair about your budget?" Dena suggested. "I bet he'd be more than on your side for the changes you want to make."

Alex shook her head with a vehement gesture. "This is *my* baby and I'll handle it my way. If I went crying to him, he'd think I can't handle my own problems and if I can't do that, how can he feel comfortable knowing I'm also supposed to be protecting him?"

The secretary nodded in agreement, seeing the logic in Alex's statement. "I'm on your side and so are most of the secretaries around here. The company certainly takes enough security precautions in the lobby and on each floor; it should allow you to do the same everywhere."

Alex laid her glasses on her desk and leaned back in her chair, resting her head back. "We'll find out, won't we?"

She hadn't expected her meeting with Walt St. Clair to be amiable, but she hadn't expected to be shot down from the moment she had stated her first project either.

"There is no reason to have all these space age gadgets set up in the parking garages when we already have them at the entrance and exit and a guard at the visitors' gate." His pompous voice set Alex's teeth on edge. "I can't imagine anyone getting past the guard or the gates, can you?" he challenged.

"Yes, I can," she replied coldly. "Not all of these perverts running around wear dirty jeans and T-shirts, Walt. They can be dressed in three-piece suits and carrying expensive briefcases. No one is allowed into the employee parking garages and the gates are only a partial deterrent. They insure that the visitors to this building use only the one level which leads directly to the lobby and a man is stationed at the gate and another at the entrance doors. Right now the assaults are happening in the employee parking areas and it's happened in three other company parking lots within the past six months. I don't intend to see it happen here." Her features were sharply etched with her anger. She added sarcastically, "Just because these attacks have been made on women in the past doesn't mean that a man might not be assaulted at some time."

"Oh, come now, Mrs. Page," Harold Morton, Walt's assistant, chuckled. He had always privately thought of Alex as a lovely woman, but a little too liberal with womens' rights as far as he was concerned. Why Mr. Templeton put her in such a position was beyond him. "Do you think a deranged woman will break into the parking garage and vent her anger on one of us?" His laughter was unkind and demeaned her suggested improvements.

Alex's eyes flashed over him with icy contempt. "Personally, Harold, I wouldn't have a damn thing to do with you, even though I have had all my shots. Of course, you can't account for some people's taste," she drawled with cold insolence. She could read their thoughts reflected on their faces. Just like a woman, get upset when she doesn't have her own way.

Alex stood up and looked at each of the five men with anger sparking in her green eyes. "It appears that nothing is going to be accomplished here." Her body was rigid with suppressed violence. "For your sake, *gentlemen,* I sincerely hope that we won't have to contend with the problem Kovack has, because our next meeting won't be as civilized. Good day." She gathered her papers together and walked out of the conference room with her head held high.

Dena looked up from her typing and saw the fury on Alex's face when she entered the office.

"Oh, oh," Dena muttered, hurriedly turning off her

typewriter and getting up from her chair to follow Alex into her office. "Let me guess, the meeting didn't go very well."

"That's the understatement of the year," she said harshly, tossing the folders on her desk, for once disregarding her old habit of neatness. "They refuse to allow me to stretch the budget this year for those cameras. They feel our security system is adequate," she snorted, clearly ready for a fight.

"Are you going to talk to Mr. Templeton about your ideas when he gets back?" Dena asked her, now a little cautious. She hadn't seen Alex in a temper like this one before.

She shook her head vehemently. "This is my battle and I'll fight it alone. And, by God, I'll win too."

The secretary nodded, never having any doubts in her belief that her boss wouldn't win. "What do you want me to do?"

Alex looked up with a grateful smile. "Research. It's going to be boring as hell, but I want a breakdown of assaults committed in buildings similar to this one with the same security measures we now have. And if there's more than one in a particular building, I want the time of day the assault occurred. The next time I go in there, I'm not going to be shot down the way I was today," she vowed, dropping into her chair. Alex picked up her telephone messages and sorted through them, now confident of her plan of attack.

A few days later, when Jared returned from his short vacation, Alex was back on the merry-go-round of short business trips to Fernwood's various offices. She said nothing about her abortive meeting with the accounting executives.

Late Thursday evening Jared pushed his chair away

from his desk and stood up to stretch his weary muscles. It was well after nine and his body was telling him that his grueling schedule was catching up with him. Deciding a quick swim was the ideal solution, he switched off the desk lamp and walked out of his office toward his private elevator.

This wasn't the first time he had chosen to take a late night swim in the gym's pool. Since it closed at eight, he knew he would have complete privacy.

Entering the men's locker room, he was surprised to hear the loud plop of a ball bouncing off a wall. Frowning with annoyance, he walked out to the counter where Max, the manager, was usually found, even at this late hour.

"Max, who has the nerve to keep you here so late?" he demanded.

Max, a balding man who resembled an aging prizefighter, grinned at his boss's assumption that no one would dare what he would do without a second thought.

"Why not take a look for yourself," he invited. "Court three."

"I will." Jared's grim face promised his wrath against the intruder. "You shouldn't have to stay late for anyone. With me, you know I always lock up when I leave."

"So does court three," Max told him, still refusing to name the unknown person. "It's just someone who has frustrations to work out."

Jared strode over to the walkway and looked down over the racquetball courts. There he could see dark hair in a braid hanging down the back and a sweatband covering the forehead. White athletic shorts bared golden legs and a pink tank top was dark with perspiration. He watched the woman pound the ball against the wall, then spin around to retrieve it off the back wall. Sensing she was under observation, she glanced up to identify her visitor.

"Working late, Mr. Templeton?" Alex called out, lifting her arm to wipe her forehead.

Jared looked over her slender body with appreciation, now seeing the curves her businesslike suits had only hinted at during the day. "I could say the same of you," he countered. "The gym closes at eight."

"I'm a special case." She added pointedly, "Just like you." The saucy grin she displayed revealed the little girl usually hidden deep in her personality. "What time is it?"

"Ten after nine."

Alex grimaced. "No wonder I feel wiped out. I've been here since a little before eight."

"Why don't you get cleaned up and I'll take you out for some dinner." Jared surprised himself by his impulsive invitation. "Knowing you, you haven't bothered eating all day."

Alex was equally surprised by his off-hand invitation. "Max said you come up here to swim sometimes." She tipped her head to one side, surveying the business suit. "Wouldn't that be more to your liking than taking one of your employees out to dinner?"

For some reason it angered him to think of her as one of his employees, yet what else could he call her? She certainly wasn't a friend. She didn't allow anyone to get close enough to her for that. Unless he counted Chris. They certainly seemed chummy enough.

Alex was considering Jared's suggestion with mixed feelings. She couldn't complain about her working conditions and she certainly had enough freedom in her job, except for the fiasco with St. Clair. At the same time, she was hungry, and she hated the thought of returning to her apartment and fixing a meal so late at night.

"I'll make a deal with you. You go take your swim while I shower and take a few minutes in the Jacuzzi," she suggested.

Jared's stern face broke into a brief smile. "Sounds good to me," he agreed. "Twenty minutes."

Alex nodded, then walked over to the door and opened a small compartment where she kept her can of balls and locker key.

She used the gym every once in a while and was able to stay late after Max realized that she cleaned up after herself and was careful to lock up when she left.

For many women, twenty minutes would have been impossible to get ready to go to dinner with a good-looking man. Not so with Alex. She took ten minutes in the Jacuzzi, then showered and changed into the clean clothes she had brought with her, a pair of black wool pants and a black and white striped silk shirt. Her hair was kept in its braid.

Alex was talking with Max when Jared walked out of the locker room. He had left his tie off and now had his jacket hooked over one finger and draped over his shoulder.

"No more late nights, Max," he admonished the man.

"The rules say no one swims alone," he corrected the younger man. "And even the Chief of Security needs protection sometimes." He smiled at Alex, who returned his warm gaze.

"You certainly have him on your side," Jared commented as they rode down in the elevator. "Max is one of the original woman haters."

"He doesn't think of me as a woman," she replied.

Jared glanced down at her with disbelieving eyes. "I find that hard to believe."

"Why don't we just walk down to Nico's?" she suggested when they reached the lobby. "That will save us taking two cars."

"For a moment back there I thought you were going to refuse my dinner invitation."

"This is a lot nicer than having to go home and fix something this late at night."

Jared felt a little annoyed that the only reason she had agreed to go out with him was to save some work for herself and not because she wished his company. She certainly knew how to tramp on a man's ego.

Nico's was a small restaurant not far from the building that catered to office workers during lunch hour and brought out the tablecloths and candles for the dinner hour. Both Alex and Jared were greeted warmly and ushered to a side booth.

Not taking time to study the menu, Alex ordered a salad and a glass of white wine.

"Cheap date," Jared joked.

"It wouldn't be good to have anything too heavy so late at night," she explained, lacing her fingers together and laying them on the table. "We have an early day tomorrow."

He smiled at her remark. "If people overheard you, they'd tend to get the wrong idea," he said silkily.

She shot him a sharp glance. "Not if I could help it."

He took a cheroot out of his cigarette case and lit it, drawing deeply. "You don't like me very much, do you?"

Alex hid the smile that threatened to appear. Did it bother Jared that much because she hadn't fallen under his spell? "Your idea of working hours might be more than many people can handle, but you're also a fair man to work for. You care about your employees. There's proof of that with your addition of the gym." Three years before, Jared had arranged for the installation of a gym for his employees, which boasted a swimming pool, three racquetball courts, and a fully equipped weight room. Alex made use of it once a week, teaching a self-defense class to the interested women employees and even to a few of the men.

Jared was even more curious to ask Alex her opinion of him as a man, but hesitated, afraid that he might not like her answer. It was true that his ego was dented a bit by the fact that she had never shown him more than superficial courtesy. That she had accepted his dinner invitation surprised him, since she usually kept him at more than arm's length. He also recalled the day when he had walked unannounced into Chris's office and found Alex and Chris talking and laughing the way old friends would. He refused to admit that he might be just the tiniest bit jealous of the easy companionship his bodyguard and secretary shared.

Sitting so close to Jared, Alex was more than aware of the musky cologne he wore that blended naturally with his body scent, leaving a woman with the impression that this man was all male. She had been around men who could exude a blatant masculinity all her life, but none who could tumble her thoughts the way Jared did. It had become increasingly more difficult to keep her mind where it belonged when she was alone with him the way she was now.

Dinner passed uneventfully, with Jared casually discussing the future of the Rams with avid football-fan Alex. They were soon engrossed in companionably arguing who had the best chance for the Super Bowl the following year.

"I'll be meeting with Rashid Kalim next Tuesday," Jared remarked casually as they relaxed over after-dinner liqueurs.

"Oh?" Alex's face sharpened with interest. She knew that Jared had been working hard for the past few months to set up this conference. "When did he finally agree to this?"

"I spoke to him this afternoon." He smiled, the action softening the craggy planes of his face. "We may have been fraternity brothers in college, but now that we're going to be on the opposite ends of the bargaining table, I'll be lucky if he concedes one point to me." His eyes gleamed with anticipation of the upcoming business battle.

"It's a pity that you're not looking forward to this," she injected dryly, noticing the air of expectancy about Jared. It was clear this was what he lived for.

"Yes, isn't it?" He grinned.

After their meal they walked slowly back to the building. Jared's hand rested lightly against the small of Alex's back, as if guiding her in their short journey. She was finding it more and more difficult to ignore the heat of his touch or the flares that erupted in the green eyes when they touched on her at odd times. This job would have been so much more safe if Jared had been short, bald, and fat! When they reached the building they entered the lobby to take the elevator to the parking garage. When they later stopped by Alex's car, she looked up with a smile.

"Thank you for dinner," she said lightly, then added in a teasing tone, "Sorry I can't ask you to come home with me, but I have a very strict mother."

Jared returned her smile, easily entering in the game. He trailed his fingertips along her shoulder, noticing the delicate bones beneath his touch. "Yes, I noticed her giving me the once-over when I came to pick you up. Not to mention the third degree your father gave me." He was surprised to see the smile disappear, leaving harshly etched lines in the delicate features.

"Yes," she said tightly, stepping away from his heated contact. "Well, good night, see you in the morning." She quickly unlocked the door and got in.

Jared remained in his spot and watched Alex drive out of the garage, wondering what he had said to wipe the smile from her face and eyes. If he had known a thoughtless remark would have done that, he certainly wouldn't have said it. Shrugging his shoulders and forgetting her problems since he had plenty of his own to worry about, he walked over to his car and prepared to go home and fall into bed for an all too brief sleep before he'd begin another working day.

The following Tuesday afternoon Jared held his meeting with several oil-rich sheikhs who were looking for new markets for their products and Alex was again on duty.

The visitors had looked at her with admiration in their dark eyes all the while amazed that a mere woman was used to protect such an important man. One man in particular, Rashid Kalim, watched Alex with something darker than mere admiration. She made sure to keep her gaze from his direction during the talks.

What Alex hadn't noticed was that Jared had seen the object of Rashid's gaze and, apparently, had not appreciated the younger man's attention on anything else than the subject of their meeting. He waited until after the men left the conference room adjoining his office before voicing his displeasure to Alex.

"You're certainly a creature of surprises, Alex," he began in a caustic tone after he had dismissed Chris.

"Oh?" She had thought she was also dismissed and was already walking toward the door when Jared's voice halted her.

"Damn it, look at me when I'm talking to you!"

Alex spun on her heel and faced Jared with rage firing her eyes. "I'll put up with your temper tantrums, Mr. Templeton, and I'll even put up with your archaic ideas that a woman's place is not necessarily in the office, but I will not, I repeat, *I will not* allow anyone to talk to me in that tone." Her voice directed icy darts at his heart. "Growing up with four brothers forced me to put up with male chauvinism all my life, and I was determined that once I graduated from the Academy, I wouldn't put up with it again, least of all from a tin god such as you!" She stood her ground, uncaring that Jared's next words would be a roar that she was fired.

To say that Jared was stunned by her fury was an understatement. Alex had always been quiet, unobtrusive, and quick to gauge the situation. She had never shown the display of temper she had just now. Deep down he admired her for her lack of fear of him, not to mention the future of her job. Jared's fierce temper was a well-known fact around Fernwood. He walked over to his desk and perched his hip on the edge.

"There have been people fired for a lot less," he began quietly. "You know that, don't you?"

"Yes." She wasn't about to apologize for her words, especially since they were the truth. Jared never saw any need to make excuses for his actions and she didn't feel she should either.

Jared shook his head, allowing a faint smile to curve his lips. "You've got guts, Alex. No one has ever had the nerve to tell me off the way you just did."

"Perhaps if more people had, you wouldn't be the egotist you are today," she continued recklessly.

Preferring not to challenge her remark, he changed the subject.

"Rashid Kalim displayed a more than passing interest in you, and I wouldn't be surprised if you hear from the man," he said in a deceptively casual voice. "Think you could put up with going out with the man, not to mention his entourage? He likes his bodyguards by the gross."

Alex shook her head, the dark hair swinging silkily against her cheek. "No, thanks."

"He's an extremely wealthy and powerful man." He dangled the gold carrot in front of her.

"So are you, but I wouldn't care to have you as a steady diet."

Jared blinked at this bit of biting honesty. He had never come across a woman who refused to succumb to his charms. The thought that Alex was immune rankled. He slowly straightened up and walked over to where Alex stood until his body was only inches away from hers.

"The navy certainly added iron to your backbone, didn't it?" He spoke softly. "I wonder if there's anything else in that body that doesn't quite go with the image?"

Alex was totally unprepared for Jared pulling her into his arms and his mouth descending to hers. Any protest she might have made was smothered by the probing thrust of his tongue and the tightening of his hold on her body.

Disjointed thoughts ran through her brain, gauging her own reactions to this unexpected attack. Her traitorous body had already melted against Jared's hard form while her arms slowly rose to circle his neck. His hands moved up and down her spine in a caressing, yet sensual, motion, then settled at the base and below to cup the firm, rounded buttocks and lift her into the cradle of his hips and feel the potent rising of his own desire.

Alex couldn't remember a man's kiss firing her the way Jared's was. Before, she had always prided herself on the ability to handle overamorous men, but not even during her marriage to Dennis had she felt such a crazy, mind-searing experience. Right now she wanted nothing more than to loosen Jared's tie and unbutton his shirt so that she could discover the silky warmth of his bare skin. She wanted to bare her own skin and feel the electric current flowing between them until they exploded in multicolored sparks.

"Ah, Alex," Jared rasped, his open mouth moving moistly over her face and circling the outline of her lips.

His teeth gently pulled on her lower lip and drew it into his mouth. "So beautiful."

His ragged words swiftly brought her back to reality. Alex's arms dropped and she quickly stepped away from the circle of Jared's potent force. It took some doing, but she soon had her breathing under control and the face she showed him betrayed none of the tumultuous thoughts running through her mind. What didn't make her feel any better was that Jared had taken that time to compose himself also. In fact, he seemed to be in better control than she.

"I hadn't realized there could be so much dynamite in that compact body." His mocking words hit her with the force of a rock slide. "I'm surprised the navy didn't make use of you as a secret weapon."

Alex's first instinct was to wipe the mocking smile off Jared's face, then she quickly restrained herself. That was what he expected her to do and she wasn't going to give him that satisfaction.

"We're going up to Pradera Alta this Saturday." He named his ranch. "You'll be going along."

For the first time, Alex looked suspicious. "Who exactly is going and why do I have to go?" This in itself was odd since she had never questioned his orders before.

Jared turned away and walked back to his desk. "Rashid will be there. Since he insists on his bodyguards going along, I will do likewise. Just pack casual clothes, you know, jeans and such. Also take some boots if you care to do some riding. All of our time won't be taken up with meetings. Oh, on your way out, would you let Chris know I need to see him." Now she was being dismissed.

If Alex hadn't had such a good hold on her emotions, her mouth might have dropped open in a very unladylike pose. Jared was acting very strangely today. First the ardent lover, now the distant cold-hearted man she was used to dealing with. Nothing was making any sense. She wondered if there was a full moon out. She nodded stiffly, then let herself out of the office and returned to her own.

Once alone in the quiet confines of her office, Alex's mind recalled the force of Jared's kiss. She wasn't surprised by her action. She had been aware of his interest in her from the very beginning, but it hadn't deterred her from taking the job. If anything, Jared presented a challenge of his own. A challenge she wasn't going to deny, but one she wouldn't dare accept either. Her only surprise was her whole-hearted response to his kiss and that worried her.

Alex remembered all too well the few years she had been married and the tragic aftermath. Memories she preferred to keep buried deeply so that they wouldn't interfere with the life she had made for herself. Funny, she hadn't thought of Dennis for a long time now. Not that she had anything against her ex-husband or that she still loved him. There might not have been any fireworks or displays of grand passion during their marriage, but there hadn't been any misery either. At least there had been no real damage to her heart. She leaned forward, massaging her temples with the tips of her fingers as if working hard to banish the headache that was beginning to appear.

"You haven't been wearing your glasses again when you read," Dena scolded, setting two aspirin and a glass of water in front of her.

"Yes, Mother," she replied wryly, picking up the pills.

"Hey, I'm only doing this to protect my own skin. You're a real terror when you get these headaches," she informed her boss.

Alex grimaced as she swallowed the two white tablets. "Mr. Templeton has decided to hold the rest of the meetings with the sheikhs at his ranch, so I'll be leaving the end of this week."

"That means no budget meeting with your favorite person in Accounting," Dena guessed.

"You've got it. I know the man will just be brokenhearted to hear the news," she said dryly. "You may as well call him and give him the glad tidings. I'll do some homework while I'm up there and really give him both barrels when I return. I can send my notes down to you with Mr. Templeton's messenger. I don't know how long I'll be gone."

Dena nodded and turned to walk out of the office. "I'll call Mr. St. Clair's office now and give him the bad news."

"At least someone's day will be made," Alex muttered, staring down at the top of her desk. She refused to admit that her confrontation with Jared had affected her in a very strange way. There was a tingling sensation in her lips that recalled the hard pressure of his mouth and she thought she could still taste the acrid tang of the cheroots he smoked. Picking up a memo, she resolutely pushed him from her mind and returned to her work.

Friday evening, Alex was more than tired when she headed for the elevator that would take her down to the parking garage. When the elevator slowed at the appropriate level and the doors silently slid open, she stepped out and frowned when she noticed some of the lights were out, giving the interior a dim, tomblike appearance.

Switching her briefcase to her left hand, Alex crossed the nearly empty garage, her footsteps loud on the concrete floor. She wasn't sure what prompted her unease, except that the prickles along her nape had always been an excellent warning device before.

She still wasn't swift enough to defend herself when a grimy hand covered her mouth and the cold steel tip of a knife teased her ribs while a man's hoarse voice sounded in her ear.

"Now, you just be nice to me, cutie, and I'll be nice to you." Stale beer fumes assaulted her nostrils. The man's hand left her mouth, reached around for her briefcase, and dropped it to the ground, then groped upward to her breast. "Get the picture?"

Alex's next moves were purely instinctive. One high heel jammed down hard on her attacker's foot while a lightning-quick jab of the elbow rammed his midriff and punched the air out of his lungs. When he dropped his hands, she immediately spun around and grasped one of the man's arms and twisted it behind his back in a bone-breaking grip.

"I suggest you be the nice one, *cutie,*" she informed him in an icy voice. "Because we are going upstairs, and don't try any tricks, because, if necessary, I can very easily break this arm." She twisted it to make her point until he cried out. "Get the picture?"

Now subdued, the man willingly accompanied her upstairs to the security office and he answered her questions while they waited for the police to arrive.

Harry Simpson, the evening shift's chief security guard, wasn't too happy at the cold glitter in Alex's eyes. It usually meant someone was in big trouble and this time it was him.

"This was inexcusable, Simpson," Alex uttered in an unladylike growl once they reached her office. "Most of the lights were out in the garage and should have been replaced immediately. Why wasn't it done?"

Harry was on the defensive at her caustic voice. "Maybe they just went out tonight," he argued, resentful that he had to answer to a woman twenty years his junior. "Besides, isn't that part of Maintenance's job?" His jaw jutted out.

"No!" Her palm slammed down on the desk top. "It's up to Security to insure that every precaution is taken to prevent what could have happened tonight. What if that slimy creep had come across one of the secretaries or one of the women managers? They could have been raped or even killed!"

"Then we're lucky that he got our lady commando, aren't we?" There was no mistaking the sneer in his voice this time.

"That's enough, Simpson!" A third voice lashed out with the cutting sting of a whip.

Alex looked up and Harry turned around just as Jared strode into the office. The dark scowl on his face wasn't pleasant to look at.

"I'm not going to be blamed for something that isn't my fault, Mr. Templeton," the guard protested with a faint whine in his voice.

"I heard you caught a mugger." Jared now turned his attention to Alex. "How did he get in?"

"He stole a parking key card," she replied crisply. "He's been hanging out where a lot of the clerical staff meet for drinks after work, and by listening in he was able to get an idea when they have to work late. He has a past record of rape and assault."

Jared's jaw tightened at the thought of what could have happened in the garage. He spun around to Harry. "Any woman who is still in this building will have an escort out to her car," he rapped out.

The man gave a sullen nod.

Jared walked forward and took Alex's arm in preparation to lead her out of the office. "That's all, Simpson," he arrogantly dismissed the man.

"What were you trying to do in there?" Alex demanded, jerking her arm from his grasp when they reached the elevators.

"Backing you up," he replied smoothly, then gently prodded her into the empty elevator car.

"You took all authority out of my hands," she accused him, her eyes narrowed like a cat ready to pounce on its prey. "I was handling the situation just fine until you walked in and took over."

"I merely echoed your sentiments regarding the security measures in the garage." Jared punched the button marked Garage. "You have my word that this won't happen again."

"Little do you know," she muttered under her breath, thinking of her arguments with Accounting. She looked up when he followed her back into the garage. "What are you doing?"

"Escorting you to your car as per my orders." His explanation was silky in response.

"I didn't realize you felt the need for protection," Alex said sarcastically.

Jared halted next to her car and stood aside as she searched the interior of her briefcase for her keys and unlocked the door. "Actually, I was thinking more in the line of protection for the mugger." His eyes danced with laughter.

"He came out very lucky," she clipped. "Any man who preys on defenseless women deserves to have the book thrown at him."

Jared inclined his head in agreement. "A driver will pick you up at nine tomorrow," he informed her. "Thank you for the escort, Mrs. Page. Have a good evening." He walked away and headed for his Maserati. Although he got inside, he didn't start the engine until Alex had backed her car out of her parking slot and drove slowly toward the exit, all the time aware of the silver car following her onto the main boulevard.

During the drive home Alex mentally reviewed her tasks for the evening. Packing would be easy; all she needed were jeans and shirts, and sweaters for the cool days. She'd also take her boots in case she did get a chance to ride, as Jared mentioned.

Her mind was still on the trip when she unlocked her front door. Her steps halted when her nape prickled again. What would it be this time?

"It's about time you got home!" A man's laughing voice banished her caution.

Alex's eyes widened at the sight of a man dressed in a naval uniform, minus the jacket, and an apron wrapped around his waist.

"Wes!" She yelped an uncharacteristic squeal as she threw herself into his arms.

"Hey!" he laughed, trying to disengage himself from her tight embrace. "Give me a chance to breathe, sis."

Alex drew back and looked up with glowing eyes at her brother's face. "When did you get in?"

"About four. Luckily I remembered I had a key to your apartment and could save the price of a hotel room. I knew you'd let me bunk here on your couch."

Her thoughts of a long visit dissolved. "I have to travel with Mr. Templeton tomorrow." Her shoulders slumped in dismay.

"Don't worry," Wes soothed. "I've been reassigned to San Diego and have to report in tomorrow anyway."

Alex's face warmed with her smile. "No more European posts?" she teased. "My, my, won't the lovely ladies in those exotic ports miss you?"

"Hey, I've got dinner pretty well ready. I'll give you the rest of my news while we eat."

"Give me five minutes." She hurried into her bedroom.

Alex's charcoal and pale gray plaid skirt and charcoal wool blazer were exchanged for a pair of well-worn jeans and an equally well-worn delapidated sweat shirt with the Naval Academy insignia on the front. When she came out,

Wes had the table set and the aroma of a ham-and-noodle casserole surrounded him.

"Smells good." She looked at the food with appreciative eyes.

"No thanks to you," he admonished. "Your cupboard was extremely bare, madam, so I had to go hunting for the nearest grocery store." He settled his six foot four inch bulk in the chair across from her.

"So tell me what you've been doing lately," Alex urged, ladling the delicious casserole onto her plate.

"After I left Italy, I flew to D.C." The smile disappeared from Alex's eyes at her brother's words. "Mom sends her love." The smile briefly appeared, then vanished again.

"And the admiral?" Her low voice betrayed a deep bitterness. "Did he also send his love?"

"Alex," Wes entreated. "Please don't dredge up old memories. They'll only hurt you again."

"Again!" she laughed harshly. "Wes, I've been hurting since I was ten years old."

Wes reached across the table and gripped her hand. "You've come a long way, Alex. You were in the top fifty of your class at the Academy, one of the up-and-coming at N.I.A., and now Chief of Security in a company that's known on an international level. You're young, beautiful, and in a position where you can have anything you want. Women envy you."

"Do they?" Her lips twisted bitterly. "Wes, every night my secretary goes home to a loving husband and two children. I come home to this." She waved her hands about the warm yet sterile surroundings. "No one envies me."

"Do you regret the divorce?" Wes asked softly.

Alex shook her head and offered him a wan smile. "No,

it was for the best all around, even if Dad was furious with me for daring to divorce a navy man."

He nodded, understanding her feelings. "Mom has a new boyfriend." He swiftly changed the subject.

"What?" This piece of news took her by surprise. When their parents had divorced ten years before, Jenny Hayden had decided to give herself a new life away from the stern confines of her husband. She remained in Washington, D.C., attending all the parties her husband had scorned, and cultivated the friendships of high-ranking government officials, but not once had any of her escorts been a member of the navy. "Who this time?"

"A senator from Montana. He's a widower and seems pretty serious about her." He grinned. "Who knows, she might give in and marry the guy."

Alex laughed, her previous sorrow now forgotten. "Good for her! She deserves all the happiness she can get."

The balance of the evening was spent in reminiscing and catching up on family news about Alex's three other brothers until Wes's jet lag caught up with him. Alex went to bed promising herself to get up early and pack then. Her visit with her favorite brother was worth the loss of sleep.

She had no warning that night. None, except the revival of old and bitter memories. She knew only that her bedside lamp was on and she was sitting upright in bed with a distressed Wes leaning over her.

"It hasn't gone away, has it?" he murmured, his hand gently brushing the tears from her cheeks. "How often does it come now?"

She shook her head. "I haven't had a nightmare in almost a year," she whispered.

He sat down on the edge of the bed and offered silent comfort.

"Thank you, Wes," she whispered against his chest, glad that he had been there when she needed him most.

"Why? You used to get me out of enough tight spots." He injected a light note. "I'm just glad I was here. No one should be alone when they hurt, Allie, not even you."

"The woman who finally gets you is going to be a very lucky lady." She smiled through her tears.

"Babe, at the ripe old age of thirty-six, I think we can guarantee my ending up as a crusty old bachelor. I'll let Troy, Nat, and Cal perpetuate the Hayden clan." He settled her back against her pillows. "Think you can get back to sleep now?" He smiled, reassured by her nod. "Then close your eyes and think of the great breakfast I'll whip up for you."

Left alone, Alex breathed deeply to dispel the tremors still running through her body. It was a long time before she could drift back into sleep.

CHAPTER THREE

The fragrance of frying bacon was better than any alarm clock. As promised, Wes had fixed pancakes and bacon for breakfast, then pushed Alex out of the kitchen, reminding her she had packing to do if she was going to be picked up at nine.

One valuable habit the military had taught her was how to pack quickly. In no time, a suitcase and tote bag were filled with essentials and she had dressed in a pale gray divided skirt, a claret-colored silk shirt, and black boots. The sides of her hair were clipped back from her face.

"You're out of dishwasher detergent," Wes announced when Alex moved her suitcase into the living room.

"What did you do, use the whole box?" she teased, knowing his fondness for believing that the more you used the cleaner things got.

Wes walked out of the kitchen, still dressed in his pajama bottoms, and sat on the arm of a nearby chair. "How long do you think you'll be at your boss's ranch?"

She shrugged. "Who knows? These meetings could be wrapped up in a matter of days or they could take a couple of weeks. Both sides of this negotiation are stubborn and refuse to back down, so I can see it ending up as a tie, if there can be such a thing with them."

"When it's over, why don't you take some vacation time and come down to San Diego. By then I should know the town well enough to find us some night life," he promised her.

"I have an idea you'll find a new girl friend before you learn anything at all about the town," she mocked him with sisterly affection. She rose from her chair when the doorbell rang.

"Templeton doesn't happen to have a woman chauffeur, too, does he?" Wes asked, looking down at his half-naked state.

"No, thank goodness, I don't think she could handle the shock." Alex was still laughing when she opened the door, a laugh which disappeared when she found Jared standing on the other side, dressed casually in jeans and a sweater.

His greeting was halted by the sight of Wes rising from his perch and lazily stretching his arms over his head. Looking back at Alex, Jared's eyes immediately frosted over.

"I apologize if I interrupted something," he began in a cold voice that was also blatantly insincere.

"No." Alex was puzzled by Jared's icy demeanor. She stepped back to allow him to enter. "Mr. Templeton, this is Commander Wesley Hayden." It was a habit of hers to use the full title when she wanted the intimidating advantage, although it didn't work with Jared.

"Commander." Jared held out his hand, but there was no friendliness in his voice.

Alex was growing a little angry by the cool reception Wes was receiving from Jared, although she noticed that her brother seemed to be only amused by Jared's actions.

"Excuse the casual attire." Wes was totally at ease.

"I've been suffering from jet lag for the past week since I left my last duty in Italy and decided to stop off here to see Alex before reporting to my new station in San Diego."

"Oh?" Jared glanced at Alex with raised eyebrows.

She stood by, confused by this cryptic conversation and resisting the urge to give her brother a good swift kick for enjoying himself too much. She had been astonished to see Jared on the other side of the door and was curious as to why he was picking her up instead of Frank. Jared turned to her, asking brusquely if she was ready. Her answer was to point silently toward her suitcase.

"Thanks for everything, Al." Wes kissed her soundly. "Give me a call when you get back to L.A. and we'll plan a wild weekend."

"Sure," she mumbled absently, still puzzled by Jared's cold attitude toward her brother.

"Shall we go?" Jared's icy voice cut through her musings.

By now Alex was angry. Just because Jared had gotten out of the wrong side of his current ladyfriend's bed didn't mean he had to take it out on her. She walked over to Wes and planted a kiss on his cheek, then retrieved her tote bag, leaving her suitcase for Jared to take.

"Don't worry, I'll lock up when I leave," Wes assured her, a wide grin on his face, and him looking as if he were enjoying a private joke.

Alex's spine was rigid with exasperation when she walked down the hallway to the elevator, a grim-faced Jared striding beside her.

"Say, Al?" Wes's cheerful voice followed them.

She looked around to see her brother holding her gun by a forefinger hooked over the trigger guard.

"You forgot your piece, sweetheart." He gave a fairly accurate imitation of Bogart.

Alex's eyes flashed sparks to him as she returned to her

apartment door and snatched the gun out of his hand to jam it inside her purse. "I'm certainly glad to see someone is enjoying this," she hissed.

"Hmm?" He squinted his eyes in Jared's direction, then looked down at her. "I'm sure you'll find out why the blizzard soon enough."

"Not soon enough for me."

Alex took her time walking back to the waiting elevator car. The ride to the ground floor was silent and their walk outside to Jared's car was equally quiet. There was a controlled violence to his actions when he tossed her suitcase into the trunk of the car.

"Are you sure you brought enough clothes?" he asked curtly once they were settled inside the Maserati.

"I'm sure your house is fully equipped with a washer and dryer," she replied coolly, taking her cue from him. "And don't worry, I'm capable of doing my own laundry," she added waspishly.

"Aren't we in a temper this morning." Jared's sarcasm only served to fuel her temper. "Obviously from a lack of sleep."

"Obviously," she snapped, recalling her restless night and the reason for it.

The Maserati sped down the street toward the freeway with a stone-faced Jared at the wheel.

"I trust that your loss of proper rest won't interfere with your duties."

Alex silently counted to ten, then began counting again. "You need not worry, Mr. Templeton. If some crank decides to take a pot shot at you, I'll be sure to be fast enough to shield your body," she stated flatly, staring straight ahead, not seeing his hands tighten on the steering wheel until the knuckles showed white.

"I suggest that the next time you have your lover over for the night, you try to get to bed, correction, to *sleep,* so that you'll be in a better mood than you are this morning," Jared advised in a derisive tone.

"My lo—" Alex half turned in her seat, all her attention now on the man seated next to her. At first she was tempted to blast him for all she was worth. The idea that Jared would assume she had men coming out of the woodwork was ludicrous. Then her sense of humor took over. No wonder Wes looked so smug! He knew exactly why Jared acted the way he did, although she couldn't understand why she hadn't guessed the reason. First a smile lifted the corners of her mouth, then a chuckle escaped, and, lastly, a laugh came from deep down.

"I'm glad you find something funny," Jared sneered.

"Oh, I do," she choked out, now laughing so hard that tears were coming out of her eyes. "I find this very funny."

"Then would you have the kindness to let me in on the joke," he demanded.

"It appears that you think Commander Wesley Hayden is more than just an old navy buddy." She was gasping for air by this time. "Your memory is slipping, Mr. Templeton, because otherwise you'd remember that my personnel records list Hayden as my maiden name."

Jared shot her a sharp glance, then quickly pulled over to the side of the street.

"He's your brother?" He still couldn't believe what he was hearing.

"One of four."

It was a good thing Alex wasn't expecting an apology, because none came. Instead, Jared grunted something like "I hope you enjoyed making a fool out of me."

"Oh, no," she corrected him in a gentle voice. "You did that all by yourself."

He stared at her as if strangulation would be too good for her. He put the car in gear and steered back onto the street. Silence hung in the air for the remainder of the drive to the airport.

They arrived at the hangar a few minutes before Rashid and his party appeared. Alex's and Jared's luggage had just been stowed away when a long black limousine rolled slowly toward them.

"Madame Page." Rashid greeted her by taking her hand and lifting it to his lips. "Ah, such a dangerous profession you have for so beautiful a woman."

Alex resisted the urge to laugh. If there was one word she wouldn't use to describe herself, it was beautiful. Her features were too sharply angled for that.

"Mr. Kalim," she murmured, inwardly amused by the dark glare Jared was directing their way.

"Shall we get aboard?" Jared suggested crisply.

"How did you rate the presidential treatment?" Chris muttered, dropping down into the seat next to Alex once they had boarded the jet.

"Who knows?" She shrugged, fastening her seat belt. "Just unlucky I guess."

"Hmm, his mood hasn't improved since last night then," he mused.

"Meaning?" She slanted a sideways glance at him.

"The Houston Handful showed up at the office late yesterday afternoon and somehow got past the receptionist," Chris said softly so that their conversation wouldn't be overheard.

"Uh-oh," she murmured.

"Oh, yes, Miss Merrilee Tanner stormed into the office and threw one huge temper tantrum." He shuddered with remembrance.

Alex remembered the lady well. Called the Houston Handful because of her well-developed figure, Merrilee had Jared's attention for all of four months. His women never lasted much longer than that. His work always came first.

"How did our fearless leader handle the lady?" Alex asked under her breath.

"The way you handle a time bomb," Chris replied. "He put on the kid gloves and agreed to meet her for dinner later in the evening."

She arched her eyebrows in disbelief. She wouldn't have thought that Jared would put up with a tantrum from anyone. Usually an act like that would have a woman quickly escorted from the building. What brought about his change of heart? That also explained his walking out with her to the parking garage last night. He had a hot date!

"She always knew how to stroke him the right way." Chris leered.

Alex glared at him, never appreciating off-color humor.

After the jet was airborne, Chris was called to the front where Jared gave him a list of instructions. When he finished, he strolled back to the seat Chris had vacated. With one hand braced on the armrest and the other on the headrest, Jared asked Alex to follow him to the rear of the jet. She nodded and unfastened her seat belt. Now it was her turn to receive her list of instructions for this course of meetings.

Jared closed the door of the bedroom behind them and leaned back while he watched Alex with narrowed eyes.

"You've got style, Alex," he drawled. "First Chris and now Rashid is after you. Who's next on your list, me?"

She spun around, not expecting this attack and disliking that light in his eyes even more. "Don't worry, you're perfectly safe from my clutches," she assured him with a feline smile.

Jared grasped Alex's arm and led her over to the bed. A gentle push set her on the edge. "Perhaps I don't want to be safe," he returned calmly, seating himself next to her. "You don't want to be either, Alex."

"Meaning?" She eyed him warily.

Jared leaned forward and nibbled a spine-tingling path along the corners of her mouth. "Very tasty," he murmured, pulling on her lower lip with his teeth.

For a moment Alex was tempted to melt against Jared, but quickly pulled away before her senses were seduced again. "I'm not in the mood for Post Office today, Mr. Templeton," she informed him in her most intimidating tone.

"I always preferred that over Spin the Bottle." Jared's fingers lightly caressed her throat and down to the neckline of her blouse. "Too many chances of the bottle pointing toward the wrong person."

"This is *not* a game!" Alex snapped, batting his wandering hands away, but he wasn't to be deterred.

His slow smile sent shivers through her. "Don't you like games, Alex?" he mused, flicking open the top button of her blouse.

"Not since the Academy," she retorted, reaching up to close the button even as Jared unfastened the next one.

His other hand pulled her blouse out of the waistband of her skirt and slid up her bare midriff until he found her bra. "Where's the clasp?" he muttered, frowning in concentration while his fingers traced a heat-producing path along the edges of the lacy cup.

If Alex had been in the right frame of mind, she probably would have laughed at the puzzled expression on Jared's face while his playful hand searched for the front clasp of the bra. "It has a back clasp with a padlock attached," she informed him sternly, wondering if he had been this persistent with his other women. It was already obvious his past experience had been with front-clasped bras, if the women wore them at all. Alex jerked away from Jared's hands and hastily pulled her blouse down, tucking the tails into the waistband of her skirt. "I haven't been manhandled like this since high school," she snapped at him while he playfully tried to "help" her. "Will you stop this! I swear, you're acting more like an adolescent than a grown man."

Jared's grin was a little too disconcerting. He reached over and flicked a stray hair away from her mouth, only to linger and trace the moist outline. Alex watched him with stormy eyes, wondering what would come next. She was fighting an inner battle to reach out and trace the enticing shape of his mouth. If she didn't do something soon, she would be lost to this sensual onslaught.

"If you don't keep your hands to yourself, Mr. Templeton, I will personally break your arm," she said softly but firmly, leaving him in no doubt that she might not think twice about it.

"You're a hard woman, Alex Page." He slowly drew back his hand, not worried about her threat. "I can only hope that the mountain air will clear your mind and give you a better perspective on things." He allowed his fingertip to trail over her cheek, then he walked out of the room, closing the door behind him.

Alex took several deep breaths to combat the anger coursing through her body. She couldn't remember ever feeling as irate as she was at that moment. Jared hadn't called her back there to discuss business with her; he only wanted a little playtime. Well, he found out soon enough that she was the wrong one to try. She only hoped that he'd keep his hands to himself for the balance of these meetings or she'd be sorely tempted to carry out her threat. A few moments later, a now composed Alex returned to the front of the jet. Chris turned and threw her a friendly grin.

"Boss give you all the dos and don'ts?"

"You could say that," she replied dryly.

"Madame Page, please join us." Rashid gestured from the round conference table he shared with Jared.

Alex noted that the only chair left was next to Jared, a fact he was well aware of, judging by the gleam in his eyes. Pasting a falsely bright smile on her lips, she took the empty chair and deliberately turned away from him to converse with Rashid in an animated fashion. What galled was that Jared easily saw through her guise.

"Yes, I agree with Alex." He spoke up, determined that she wouldn't forget his presence. He leaned forward and firmly planted his hand on her knee, stroking her skin.

Two can play at this! She fumed at this blatant attempt to display ownership. Still talking and not sparing a glance in Jared's direction, Alex brought her boot heel down on his foot just above the toes. She had to give him credit. A brief glance showed that his expression hadn't even changed under her punishing boot, although his hand remained on her knee just under the hem of her skirt. Alex merely leaned forward and put all her weight on the one foot. A moment later Jared's hand slowly removed itself from her knee, and just after that she lifted her foot.

"Is something wrong, Mr. Templeton?" she asked, gazing at him with false concern.

"Not a thing, Mrs. Page." He clearly admired her subtle retaliation.

There wasn't time for further word games, as the announcement came forth that they would be landing soon.

Alex was the first to disembark the jet at the tiny airport.

"I feel like the lead man for a bunch of gangsters," she muttered to herself as several men approached the jet.

"Hello, Tim," Jared greeted one of the men who looked as if he had just stepped off a western movie set with his dusty boots and jeans, faded wool shirt, and Stetson in one hand.

"Mr. Templeton." His lined, weather-beaten face was creased in a broad grin. He glanced curiously at Jared's party, in particular, Alex.

Jared made the necessary introductions and seemed to take great pleasure in explaining Alex's function.

"Well, hell, Mr. Templeton." Tim scratched the gray strands of hair on his head. "Who's gonna protect the lady?"

"You don't need to worry about me." Alex smiled, used to this confusion when her profession was revealed.

"Is there a reason why we're out here in the midst of nothing, my friend?" Rashid asked Jared.

"The only way you can reach my ranch is by Jeep. Tim and the others are here to drive us up there." Jared took charge and instructed who would sit in which Jeep. Alex was relieved to be put with Chris and one of Rashid's bodyguards. The other shared a Jeep with Jared and Rashid while Rashid's secretary sat in the last Jeep with the luggage. In no time the Jeeps were bumping along the highway.

"No wonder why I'm a city boy," Chris grumbled, looking around at the barren countryside. "It looks as if all you can do around here is listen to the grass grow, if that."

Alex shot him an exasperated look. "Some peace and quiet won't hurt any of us after the wild lives we lead in the city," she informed him in a dry voice.

"Wild lives, don't I wish!" he groaned.

Alex gathered her wool blazer more closely about her. She had forgotten how even closed Jeeps can be drafty. She turned to ask the driver the whereabouts of the ranch, but didn't receive a satisfying answer.

"What did I tell you?" Chris mumbled. "We're in the middle of the wilderness."

Soon enough, the Jeeps turned off onto a side road whose gateposts held a sign stating PRADERA ALTA, which the driver translated as "high meadow" in Spanish.

"Mr. Templeton's grandmother is a descendant of one of the founding Spanish families," he explained. "She lives in Santa Barbara now. Quite a lady too." He chuckled.

Alex settled back in her seat and surveyed the trees, bared of their leaves in mid-winter. Even in this barren land she saw a stark beauty that soothed her mind. Without warning, the memory of Jared's hands on her naked flesh intruded into her thoughts. Her body began to ache, wanting the sure caress that right now was only in her mind. She hurriedly turned her head, looking out the window, needing a diversion to control her heightened senses. What was happening to her? No man had ever jumbled her mind before, and she didn't intend Jared to be the first.

Twenty minutes later the Jeeps pulled in front of a sprawling one-story adobe ranch house. Alex scrambled out of the Jeep with a grumbling Chris close behind her.

"If I don't sit down for the rest of the week, it will be too soon," he moaned.

"Shut up," she ordered mildly, looking around with interest. She turned when the front door opened and a small gray-haired woman walked out onto the veranda.

"You're late," she brusquely informed Jared, resting her hands on tiny hips.

"Hello, Mavis." He greeted her with obvious affection, throwing his arms around her for a bear hug.

"None of that now," she scolded, drawing away from him, but the twinkle in her eyes belied her words. Her dark eyes surveyed the group, hesitating only once on Alex, then moving on.

"Are the rooms for my guests ready?" Jared asked.
"Naturally," she snapped, although the smile never left her eyes. This was clearly no normal servant/employer relationship, as Mavis treated Jared like her son.
"My housekeeper, Mavis," he explained to the others. "She'll show each of you to your rooms."
As they entered the house, a fine misting rain fell, giving the countryside a gray cast. They were led into the living room, which boasted fine antiques much to Alex's delight.
"Mr. Kalim." Mavis pronounced his name with a broad *a.* "Would you come with me please?"
"Would you care for some coffee?" Alex spun around, disconcerted to find Jared standing next to her.
"Exactly why am I here?" she demanded without preamble. "You don't need bodyguards in such an isolated place."
"Rashid has his."
"I'm sure if you had asked him nicely, he would have shared them with you." She kept her voice low, anxious that no one overhear her.
"Ah, but I preferred to have my own nearby," he murmured, keeping his eyes on the enticement of her heaving breasts. Without warning his voice turned serious and impersonal. "There are reasons why we're conducting the meetings here instead of my office."
"Then I should have been the first to know them."
"You will, after lunch," he said cryptically. "Would you care for some coffee?"
Alex shook her head. "All I want is a hot shower." Her mint-green eyes narrowed. "I feel grubby."
The white lines around Jared's mouth told her that her thrust hit home.
"Yes." His voice was hoarse. "I know just the feeling."
Alex paled under the unexpected attack. Well, she couldn't complain, could she? All Jared had done was

defend his pride the best way he could. Past experience had her see him use a few well-chosen words to flay a supposedly self-assured man to ribbons. Just the way her father would deal with someone. Alex wasn't aware that her eyes had suddenly clouded over and her jaw had tightened. Jared was alternately puzzled and concerned by her abrupt withdrawal.

"Alex?"

Slowly the eyes cleared and the taut muscles relaxed. She tipped her head back and smiled at him, a narrow, bitter smile.

"You have it down pat, Mr. Templeton," she said softly. "You missed your calling. You should have been in the navy. You would have had a brilliant career." She turned away and walked swiftly toward Chris.

Jared watched her with confused eyes. Although Chris didn't seem to notice anything unusual, he was quick to see that Alex's voice was pitched a shade higher than normal and her gestures weren't natural. Again he fought the urge to go over and shake the truth out of her, to demand the reason for these chilling withdrawals. He also suffered from an irritating jealousy that Alex could act so natural and carefree with Chris while she was tense and abrupt with him. Except . . . His lips curved with the memory of her slender warmth curled against him. What would it be like to have that warmth all night? He turned away and cursed himself for these tormenting thoughts that only served to heighten his frustration.

When Alex was shown to her room, she was surprised to be steered toward a different wing of the house than the others had been taken to.

"Aren't the others in a different wing?" she asked Mavis.

The housekeeper nodded as she drew back the drapes

to reveal a breathtaking view of the mountains. "Mr. Templeton thought you'd be more comfortable here."

Away from the men is more like it, Alex thought to herself, setting her tote bag on the bed. Her suitcase had already been delivered to her room and was sitting on the carpet next to the bed.

"Lunch is at one," Mavis told her. "There's plenty of towels in the bathroom. If you need anything, just say so."

Alex shook her head. "I don't think I will. Thank you."

After Mavis left her, Alex busied herself unpacking and putting her clothes away. She looked around the bedroom, finding the Spanish theme repeated in the dark wood four-poster and heavy dresser with an ornate mirror hung above. A painting of a Spanish castle hung over the bed and an Indian print blanket partially covered another wall. The brick-colored bedspread was heavy cotton, yet soft to the touch. The bathroom was completely modern, including a separate shower cubicle next to the bathtub.

Alex was surprised by the simplicity of the furnishings in the house. She had heard that Jared's house in Brentwood was very plush compared to this. This was a home and another side of the man she hadn't seen before. She had an idea that her time here would be very informative, if not dangerous to her peace of mind.

Without warning Alex's knees suddenly buckled and she collapsed onto the edge of the bed. Was she fighting some type of physical attraction for Jared?

"God help me," she whispered, looking down at her clenched fists lying in her lap. While she did an excellent job of protecting other people, could she perform that same duty for herself, not just her body, but her emotions as well?

CHAPTER FOUR

A few moments before one o'clock Alex returned to the living room to find everyone already there. After seeing Jared standing away from the others talking to Rashid in low tones, she felt comfortable enough to join Chris, who had been valiantly attempting a conversation with Rashid's two bodyguards and male secretary.

"Their only other main language is French," he muttered to Alex, "the only subject I flunked in school. The secretary can understand English; he just doesn't speak it very well. I hope we're having lunch soon."

As if hearing Chris's fervent prayer, Jared glanced up and suggested they move into the dining room.

Lunch was simple, but filling. Mavis served them chicken with parsley dumplings and apple cobbler for dessert. Jared had been his charming self, including asking Alex to play hostess and sit opposite him at the table.

During the meal she experienced Rashid's dark speculative eyes on her. She wondered, with a spark of humor, how he'd react if she told him that she knew his unspoken question was if she'd like to live in a harem.

"If you gentlemen will excuse us, I need to go over a few points with Alex." Jared was still the gracious host when they left the table after the meal.

"Obviously he didn't get it all said on the plane," Chris commented in a low voice.

"Obviously," Alex murmured, moving to follow Jared into his study.

"Have a seat, Alex." He gestured toward a soft leather chair while he perched himself on the edge of his desk.

"I hope I now get to hear the details." There was an ironic twist to her words. "It seems we didn't get down to business on the flight up here."

Without bothering to reply, Jared twisted his body so that he could pick a sheaf of papers up from the desk. "These will explain why we're having the meetings here." He tossed the papers onto her lap.

Alex carefully studied each crudely scrawled note. A cold lump settled in the pit of her stomach at the meaning of the words. She had seen enough of these letters in the past that they shouldn't bother her, but they always did. "It's the same group who's been writing all those letters and sending those cassette tapes for the past few months," she commented, working hard to remain objective. "Why didn't you have me contact the police about this new one?" she asked him, raising her head to stare at him. "These people mean business. They're not your run-of-the-mill cranks. This letter proves it."

Jared shook his head. "I couldn't afford to advertise these negotiations any more than necessary."

"Afraid the price might be raised too high for even you?" she taunted softly.

His face darkened at her words. "You, of all people, should know better, or didn't you read those notes carefully enough?"

Alex had. The description of what the writer wanted to

do to Jared and Rashid were all too clear and the thought of such a thing sickened her.

"Therefore, the meetings were scheduled to be held here," she murmured, now understanding why Jared had been willing to give up the sanctity of his ranch. This location had never been suggested before for any important negotiations.

"This has always been my refuge from the fast lane, Alex," Jared disclosed quietly, leaning forward to emphasize his point. "For now, it's the same as a hideaway for me."

Alex's eyes were riveted on his face and the play of emotions that crossed the strong features. He really hated bringing them here! She suddenly longed to reach out and erase the lines furrowing his forehead, but now wasn't the time for comfort.

"Do you think they'll find out about the negotiations being held here?" She kept her voice matter-of-fact.

He shrugged. "All I can do is hope not. The company needs the oil from those new wells and Rashid is now ready to bargain." He straightened up and walked around to drop into his desk chair, his voice impersonal. "We'll begin at nine each morning, break for two hours for lunch, and then reconvene until evening. Although we're in a more relaxed atmosphere here, we'll still keep these talks on a formal footing. You and Rashid's men will take turns staying with us or remain nearby."

"I'd like to go over the grounds," she murmured, remaining just as aloof. "Could a horse be made available for my use?"

"Certainly. I'll let Tim know."

Now there was only uneasy silence surrounding them. Alex racked her brain. This was something new for her—a loss of words around Jared. They never had a problem talking before.

"Hell, isn't it?"

She looked up to find him watching her with a wry expression in his eyes. "For once we can't talk to each other in a natural manner." Jared lit a cheroot and drew on it deeply.

"It's all your fault," she blurted out, then wished she could take back her childish accusation.

"I don't know about that," he drawled. "I suggest you take a good look in the mirror sometime because you're going to find yourself looking at a very sexy lady."

Now Alex did relax and laugh in a natural manner. "You better get your eyes checked, Mr. Templeton. My father said that all that saved me from being homely were my cheekbones."

Jared's eyes roamed over the almond-shaped green eyes, a nose that women consulted a plastic surgeon to possess, the high cheekbones, a well-shaped mouth with the slightly fuller lower lip that could so easily curve into a stomach-stopping smile. She was too slender for her height, but he knew that was a result of too few regular meals and working nonstop.

"Your father is a fool," he said softly.

Alex resisted the urge to shift in her chair under his close scrutiny. "If there isn't anything more, Mr. Templeton, I'd like to prowl around the grounds." She endeavored to replace this talk on a formal level.

She thought a bleak expression flickered in his eyes, but it disappeared before she could tell for sure.

"I'll let Tim know you'll be down at the stables within the hour or so." Jared picked up his pen, indicating the conversation was closed.

As promised, a bay mare was waiting for Alex when she found her way to the stables built not too far from the house. Tim greeted her with a ready smile and cheerfully gave her directions for surveying the immediate grounds.

In no time Alex had adjusted her body to the mare's easy walk. The light rain had stopped, leaving silver droplets on the winter-bare trees and bushes. She soon forgot her reason for her ride and lost herself in the delight of the desolate, yet beautiful, countryside. She could easily see why Jared preferred this home to his house in Brentwood for rest and solitude. Here he was one with nature. Even as she lost herself in the stark beauty surrounding her, her keen eyes were noting each hill, gauging the distance to the ranch house and accessibility from the outside.

Outside, she laughed softly to herself. If someone had read her thoughts, they would assume the land was hers, already thinking of everywhere else as the outside.

Alex enjoyed her ride so much she didn't return to the house until dusk.

"The boss is all fired up, wondering where you've been," Tim greeted her.

"That's nothing new." She dismounted and handed the reins to the man.

"Mavis said dinner would be at six thirty," he called after her, receiving a nod in reply.

Alex stretched her arms over her head as she entered the house, anticipating a hot bath to soak the aches away. She had forgotten how long it had been since she had ridden.

After discarding her clothes, she ran her bath, adding scented bath oil to the hot water. She pinned her hair on top of her head and stepped into the tub sighing with delight.

Alex soaked in the water and wondered why this switch in Jared's personality. The funny thing was, if she hadn't liked him touching her, why hadn't she handed in her notice? But where else could she find a job with the extra benefits she had now? She also had a reckless streak in her and couldn't help but wonder how far Jared would try to go with her. All she knew was if he informed her it was either his bed or her job, she'd cheerfully tell him what he could do with the job . . . wouldn't she?

Knowing dinner would be served soon, Alex stepped out of the tub and wrapped a towel around her, patting the moisture from her shoulders.

"Damn," she murmured when she realized she had left her underwear in the bedroom.

She walked into her bedroom and stopped short when she found Jared lounging on the bed. His eyes gleamed at her near-nude form.

"Aren't you lost?" She quickly regained her composure.

"Not now." A scrap of turquoise lace dangled from his fingertips. "Why, Mrs. Page, I hadn't realized you wore such sexy lingerie. A remarkable insight into your personality." There was a hint of laughter in his voice.

"Give me that!" Alex hissed, snatching the panties out of his hand.

"I suppose you want this too." His other hand magically produced the matching wispy bra. "You really don't need to wear one, Alex."

"You're disgusting!" she accused him, reaching out for the sheer bra, but Jared held it out of her reach. "Give it to me, Jared!" In her anger she unwittingly used his first name.

A slow smile appeared and his voice turned into silken honey. "I'd certainly like to," he murmured with sensual emphasis.

Alex's face burned at his intimate suggestion and her hand lashed out to wipe his smile from his face. Just before her hand connected with his cheek, her wrist was gripped and she was pulled off-balance only to fall ungracefully across the bed. Jared's eyes glittered with anger as he leaned over her.

"Keep on struggling, Alex," he advised sardonically.

"The precarious knot in your towel is almost undone anyway."

"Let me go!" she blazed, vainly trying to strike out with her other hand, but Jared easily evaded her blows.

"Some bodyguard you are," he chided. "You're going to have to practice, darling. Your timing is just a shade off."

Now incensed, Alex began calling Jared every name in the book, but it only served to amuse him.

"So that's what they taught you in the navy." Gripping both her wrists in one hand, the other trailed slowly up her leg to her knee then moved over the towel until it reached the tuck, which had come undone during her struggles.

Alex held her breath, waiting for what would come next.

Jared loosened the towel and pushed the ends away to reveal her still-damp body. A sharp hiss escaped his lips as he gazed downward.

"You have a lovely body, Alex," he murmured. "One that should be worshiped—often."

"I didn't realize this was to be part of my duties, Mr. Templeton." Her face was a frozen mask.

"I liked it better when you called me Jared." His lips found the sensitive spot just behind her ear while his fingers explored every inch of her breasts with delicate precision.

Alex swallowed, already feeling a searing heat course through her body at his butterfly touch. She silently cursed him for bringing these sensations to the surface.

"You're thinking again," he accused her mildly as his tongue traced a feathery path along the lines of her throat. Even as he spoke, his voice roughened with the need that pulsated through his body. His hand had traveled down over her waist to her hips and around to the soft inner thigh.

It took a great deal of concentration for Alex to keep back her gasp at his probing, intimate touch.

"Touch me, Alex," he demanded thickly, releasing one of her hands and bringing it to his chest. "Show me you're capable of passion too." His head lowered and his mouth covered hers in a soul-destroying kiss. She couldn't keep back her moans when his head lowered even farther to fasten his teeth on a sensitive nipple and lightly graze it.

Her fingers busily unbuttoned Jared's shirt and tore it loose from the waistband of his jeans. She undulated under his hard body and arched up, demanding that his need be hers.

"Let's not go in to dinner," Jared suggested raggedly, covering her face with heated kisses even as his fingers teased her moist warmth.

"We can't." She found it hard to form words by now. Her own hands were occupied with fumbling with his belt buckle even as she spoke words she didn't want to believe. At that moment she wanted him badly. "They'll miss us."

His chuckle danced on her nerve endings. "Envy us, perhaps, but not really miss us."

Jared's arrogant assumption was as good as a cold shower on Alex's heated flesh. Holding on to her last threads of sanity, she pushed him away and drew her towel around her.

"If you're trying to make a point about a physical attraction for each other, forget it," she told him in a cool voice.

"A moment ago you were willing to go along with that so-called point," he reminded her.

"I have a suggestion, Mr. Templeton." Her voice was dangerously soft. "You leave right now and stay away from me and I won't say anything about what just happened. You come near me again and you'll wish you hadn't."

Jared took his time standing up and tucking his shirt into his jeans without bothering to button it. "In the end, spitfire, *you'll* be the one coming to me." He flashed her a wolfish grin. "It's obviously been a long time since a man has made love to you, and so far I've served you only the appetizer. Soon enough you're going to crave the entire meal."

"Get out!"

Jared walked to the door but turned back to her before he opened it. "Satisfy my curiosity. What was your husband like? Was he so navy macho that you felt the need to divorce him?"

He was surprised by the bleak voice that replied. "Dennis is the kindest, most gentle man you could know. A good man, too good for me, so I did him a favor; I gave him his freedom." She slowly lifted her face. "Are you satisfied now?"

Jared's eyes didn't leave the pain-etched features. Without saying a word, he turned and opened the door and walked out.

After a few moments Alex slowly pulled her towel closer to her chilled body. In the space of a very short time, Jared had done an excellent job of starting to destroy her defenses. If she wasn't careful, she would be thrown into a pit so deep she'd never be able to get out. With slow, fumbling movements, she slid off the bed and began to dress. Her turquoise underwear was stuffed back into a dresser drawer. She doubted she would ever be able to wear them again without recalling the sight of Jared's lean fingers holding them up.

Alex made sure to join the group a few moments before dinner would be announced. When she hesitated under the archway leading into the living room, her eyes were captured by Jared's hooded gaze. He raised his glass in a silent, mocking salute and drank deeply of the contents.

"Madame Page." Rashid appeared at her side and lifted her hand to his lips. "You look lovely, as always." His dark eyes appreciated her burgundy velvet floor-length skirt and white ruffled blouse. She had coiled her hair on top of her head, emphasizing the delicate features.

"Here." Jared approached her and held out a glass. "I'm sure you need this," he added with a sardonic grin.

Alex's eyes shot sparks as she accepted the glass, not seeing Rashid's amusement at the electric tension between them.

"It wasn't so long ago, my friend, that I would have thought nothing of offering to buy your woman." Rashid turned to Jared.

"The price would have been very high," he replied lightly, ignoring Alex's gasp of outrage. "She's quite a spitfire."

"I am no man's woman," she stated through clenched teeth.

Jared continued grinning. "She's stubborn too."

Not caring to indulge in this ridiculous conversation any further, Alex whirled away and stalked over to Chris, who was talking to Rashid's secretary and two bodyguards. He gave her a puzzled glance, but before he could ask her what the problem was, Mavis walked in to say dinner was on the table.

When they entered the large dining room, Jared steered Alex toward the chair she had used during lunch.

"You can play hostess again," he explained.

"And you know what you can do," she murmured acidly, slipping into the chair he held out for her.

Alex decided that too many of Mavis's meals would indeed turn her into a pudgy lady if she wasn't careful. Yet she couldn't resist the mouth-watering pork roast and delicately seasoned scalloped potatoes au gratin with blueberry pie following.

Conversation during the meal was kept informal, as if the two principals had already agreed that this wasn't the time to discuss business. She smiled and replied when spoken to, but had no idea what she had said. After dinner, Jared and Rashid excused themselves in order to engage themselves in a game of chess in Jared's study.

"Think we could talk these suckers into a game of five-card stud?" Chris murmured to Alex.

"With our luck, they could be card sharks." At that moment she wanted nothing more than to crawl into bed and hopefully catch up on the sleep she had lost the night before. "Go ask. Just don't try any stupid signals in my direction. I'm pretty sure that Jamil carries the Middle Eastern version of the Bowie knife on his person."

Chris considered her words with a thoughtful frown. Jamil, a tall man in his late twenties, already sported a sinister-looking scar along one cheek. Alex had noticed him watching her closely that afternoon during lunch, but a few sharp words from Rashid had kept the man at a polite distance.

Chris was saved from making a decision when Jamil, speaking slowly in heavily accented English, explained he would walk about the grounds and then retire. Yussef, the second bodyguard, and Moustafa, Rashid's secretary, also excused themselves.

"Backgammon?" Chris turned back to Alex.

"Why not?"

Alex was able to forget her worries for the next few hours between backgammon and Chris's insane comments during the game.

"I thought old salts played only poker," he challenged after she had won again.

"I learned poker when I was five. I've only been playing this for the past few years," she replied demurely.

"I'm sure glad I didn't suggest strip poker."

Alex laughed at Chris's sigh of relief—a laugh which she abruptly choked on when she saw Jared and Rashid standing in the doorway. Jared appeared angry while a faint smile of amusement played about Rashid's lips.

"There's nothing to worry about with him, Jared," Rashid murmured.

"I don't know what you mean." He made an effort to slowly unclench his hands.

Rashid laughed softly. "I can only hope that you will be as transparent during our negotiations, because I can then be assured I will make a lot of money. Now, I will bid you a good night." He turned away to head for his room.

"I don't suppose you persuaded Mr. Kalim to agree to your price over a hot game of chess?" Chris greeted their boss.

"We should be so lucky." Jared took a healthy swallow of Scotch from the glass he held in one hand. His green eyes captured Alex's gaze, which persisted in looking through him instead of at him. At that moment he wanted to shake her into awareness of him as a man—a man who wanted to discover the rest of the secrets he had only just begun to learn earlier that evening. A harsh note entered his voice. "I hope the two of you won't be too bored." Without another word, he turned and walked out of the room.

Chris watched Jared's leavetaking with puzzled eyes before he turned back to Alex. "Alex, did you and the boss have an argument or something?" he asked curiously. "He was looking strangely at you during dinner, not to mention just now."

With a great deal of effort, she was able to produce a semblance of indifference. "Did he? I think he's just concerned about these negotiations." Seeing that Chris was ready to interrogate her further, she rose from her chair. "I think I'll go to bed. It's been a long day."

Chris also stood up and leaned over to drop a light kiss on her forehead. "Just remember, I'm here when you need a friend," he said softly.

"Thanks, friend." She laid her palm against his cheek. "Good night."

Even with her lack of sleep the night before, Alex found it difficult to drop off. She rolled over onto her stomach and punched her pillow into a comforting shape. There was only one problem. It wasn't the shape her body was unconsciously seeking.

Since the meetings wouldn't begin until Monday, Sunday was spent quietly.

Jared, Rashid, and one of Rashid's bodyguards drove into Santa Barbara for some sightseeing. Alex spent the afternoon in the study making use of Jared's calculator and going over the figures for her annual budget. Every tap of the total button and the displayed figures brought her closer to blowing her temper.

"Damn St. Clair for this," she muttered savagely, picking up the sheets of paper and crumpling them before throwing them into the wastebasket. She made a mental note to call Dena in the morning with fresh instructions.

Expelling a weary sigh, she pulled her glasses off and dropped them on the desk. She leaned back in the chair and massaged her temples, hoping to get rid of her headache before it grew to gigantic proportions. She was glad that Jared wasn't around to increase it.

It was agreed that one bodyguard would remain in Jared's study with the two men and their secretaries while one would patrol the front of the house and the other the back.

Alex first made a quick phone call to Dena, brusquely informing her to type up the purchase requisitions for the security cameras, send them up for her signature, then snowball them through Accounting. She wanted those cameras installed within ten days and Dena had her permission to use her name and bully anyone possible to get the job done.

"It's nice to know that you'll be standing behind me in the unemployment line if this falls through," Dena said ruefully.

"It won't," Alex assured her in a hard voice.

After her phone call she went into the kitchen for a cup of coffee and wandered outside to the porch.

Gone were the crisp businesslike suits. This morning she wore jeans tucked into black leather boots and a royal blue heavy challis man-tailored shirt topped by a down vest. Her gun and holster were fitted under her vest so that nothing could be seen. Settling herself in a rocking chair, she swung her legs up to rest crossed ankles on the porch railing.

"Now all we need is the James boys to ride slowly up the trail," she murmured, sipping the hot brew, all the time gazing at the surrounding hills. A pair of binoculars sat on the floorboards in case any unfamiliar movements caught her attention.

Alex had learned the fine art of patience a long time ago. By blanking her mind of all thoughts, the time passed without pain or boredom until lunch was announced. Afterward she took her place beside Chris in the study.

"What's the score?" she asked softly, keeping her eyes from Jared's rugged figure dressed casually in jeans and a wool shirt.

"Even," he replied under his breath. "Neither is giving an inch."

"Wonderful." She expelled a deep breath. "At this rate, we'll be celebrating Christmas up here."

Chris arched a teasing brow. "Not too much faith in our leader," he chided. "This is only the first day. Things won't get hot until the end of the week at least."

That afternoon Alex sat in the soft leather chair and listened with half an ear to the conversation between the two men. What came through, instead, was the deep tones of Jared's voice, velvet, edged with steel, whose coverings could be ripped off in a matter of seconds. One moment he was amused indulgence, the next, a caustic wit that could tear a man to shreds. She had to admire his quick-minded intelligence and immediate grasp of the situation. Without it, he wouldn't have gotten to where he was today.

For the first time, Alex listened to two men who were evenly matched in all ways. Chris was right. These negotiations could prove to be very long.

Several times during the course of the afternoon, Jared's eyes locked with Alex's but neither betrayed their thoughts. Both were masters of their own kind of disguise, but the other was beginning to see below the camouflage. It was only a matter of time before all the outer trappings would be ripped away to reveal the real person beneath.

A week later Jared and Rashid were still deadlocked. During one trying afternoon session Alex took an urgent telephone call from Dena.

"Oh, Alex, it's all broken loose around here!" Dena wailed before Alex barely had a chance to greet her secretary.

"St. Clair found out about the cameras?" she guessed.

"Found out? The man almost had a coronary," she continued. "He's threatened to tell Mr. Templeton how we both overstepped our bounds. We'll be without jobs by the end of the week."

The gears in Alex's brain were already clicking away. Now was the time for a showdown, and she cursed Jared for her being here instead of at Fernwood confronting the head of Accounting with her facts and figures.

"Did you get that report compiled yet?"

"Yes, you'll get it in the morning." Dena took a deep breath. "Alex, I'm scared. Mr. St. Clair has a lot of power around here."

Alex smiled grimly. "Don't worry, Dena, no matter what happens, I won't let you be thrown to the wolves. Do you trust me?"

"More than I trust me."

"Then say the hell with St. Clair and take the rest of the day off," she instructed. "The man wants a fight and he's going to get one." The steel that threaded her voice was an echo of her father if she had but chosen to recognize it. Alex had been taught from an early age never to back down from an adversary. This was one time when those teachings would come in handy.

The report arrived with Jared's messenger along with the purchase requisitions with a scrawled "Not Approved" across them along with the initials, W.S.C. Alex muttered brief but concise aspersions on Walt's character, then threw the requisitions into the wastebasket.

She wasn't surprised when Jared asked to see her in his study after dinner that evening. The grim lines etching the corners of his mouth warned her of what would come.

"I was certainly right when I said you have guts, Alex," Jared began without preamble once the study door was closed behind them. "I had a very interesting telephone call from Walt St. Clair this afternoon."

"Oh?" She dropped into a chair.

Jared shot her a dark glare. It was obvious that he was

barely able to keep his temper in check. "To begin with, he's accusing you of using your so-called relationship with me to get all your money-spending proposals pushed through," he sneered.

She may have appeared relaxed on the outside, but inwardly she was a jungle cat ready to pounce. "My opinion of the man would most probably burn your ears," she drawled.

"I doubt any more than some of the names you called me not that long ago." The cold rage on Jared's face would have quelled a lesser opponent. "I don't appreciate people making those kinds of insinuations, and I especially don't appreciate the nasty chuckles that accompany them."

"Then tell him to get off my back," she stated baldly.

"*You're* the one who's making trouble, Alex, not Walt!" he roared.

"Wrong!" she shouted back, jumping to her feet. "He doesn't believe in women making management decisions and he opposes me every chance he gets. I don't intend to let him oppose me on something as important as these security measures. We've already had one attempted assault. What happens next time if the proper precautions haven't been taken?"

"We've already spent a great deal of money for new security measures in the past year, so we should be adequately protected, shouldn't we?" Jared argued.

"Are we?" Her eyes flashed dangerous sparks. She turned around and walked toward the door.

"I'm not finished," he ground out.

Alex turned her head to deliver a scathing look. "I am," she snapped, opening the door and slamming it behind her.

As always, there was no warning to herald the disturbance of her sleep that night.

Her body tensed under the covers and keening moans were torn from her throat. Fingers clutched the bedcovers in a frantic attempt to banish the horror.

"Alex, Alex!" The voice insisted on intruding but the dark shadows were strong this time and unwilling to give up their victim.

"No!" She sat up in bed, wildly grabbing the figure seated on the edge of the bed beside her. "Don't let them get me!" she pleaded, a far cry from the cool, self-assured woman she showed to the world.

Jared wrapped his arms around her and spoke quietly into her ear until her sobs gradually subsided to ragged sniffs. He had been sleeping soundly in his room at the end of the hall when Alex's moans and cries had awakened him. When he entered her room, he hadn't expected to see her body thrashing wildly in its sleep-filled torment. The sight tore through him.

"It's just a bad dream, Alex," he crooned. "Nothing more."

"No." She shook her head emphatically. "You don't understand."

"Then tell me," Jared suggested, still continuing to speak softly. "What is it?" Leaning back slightly, he was surprised to see tears streaming down her cheeks. He frowned, realizing she was speaking the truth. This was more than just a bad dream for her. "Alex, what is it?"

Although she found a measure of comfort in his arms, she didn't trust him enough to reveal her inner fears.

"As you said, it was just a bad dream," she replied in a distant voice. "I'm sorry I disturbed your sleep."

Jared's jaw turned to granite at her prim "thank you." "It was more than just a nightmare. You're frightened of something," he gauged.

"Doesn't anything ever frighten you?" she challenged.

"Yes, you," he replied without hesitation. "You frighten me, no, you more than frighten me; you scare the hell out of me. I figure I'll wake up one morning and discover you were nothing more than a figment of my imagination."

Alex was silenced by this intense and all too candid reply. The atmosphere in the room was just a little too intimate with her in her nightgown and Jared wearing only a pair of jeans, his lightly tanned chest bare save for its sprinkling of hair narrowing down to disappear in the waistband of his jeans. She hadn't wanted to think how the musky scent of his skin had filled her nostrils or how the feel of the crisp hairs on his chest tickled her nose when he had held her close to him. The comforting part of his embrace was over as far as she was concerned.

"You're lying," she finally managed to whisper.

His fingers toyed idly with her nightgown strap. "Am I?" he asked lazily. "I figure when morning comes, I'll discover that my bodyguard is really Max."

A reluctant smile tugged at the corners of her lips. How could she laugh when the slightly rough fingertips were caressing her bare skin and finding their way down to the deepest point of her nightgown's neckline. "I'd like to go back to sleep now," she said pointedly.

He flashed her a crooked grin. "Great idea."

Now fully awake and temporarily immune to his touch, she lifted one hand and circled her fingers around his wrist. "Jared, go away," she purred, then adroitly twisted her hand around until she had a bone-breaking grip on his fingers.

He winced even as he replied wryly, "Okay, you've made your point. Though how I'll explain the bruises in the morning, I'll never know."

"Good night, Jared."

He nodded and stood up. "It's a step in the right direction. At least you're using my first name now."

After he left she huddled under the covers, beginning to wonder if she might not have been better off staying in the navy after all.

The next morning Jared detained Alex just as they left the dining room after breakfast.

"Did you sleep all right after I left?" he asked softly.

"Naturally."

For a moment Jared's eyes darkened with some undefinable emotion. "If you need to talk, I'll be willing to listen, anytime."

This gentle side could soon prove to be her undoing. Where Dennis and anyone else who had tried to banish these dreams had always failed, Jared could succeed. Deep down she believed that, but she didn't want him to have that hold over her. Now there weren't any signs of the fear that had been on her face during the early morning hours.

"There's nothing to talk about. Now, if you'll excuse me, I have some of my own work to do before your meetings." She walked away, leaving a puzzled Jared behind.

CHAPTER FIVE

By Friday of the third week Alex's carefully controlled patience was beginning to run out. Her daily telephone calls to Dena weren't helping her peace of mind either. Deep down in the very bones of her body she had a feeling something was going to happen.

Two days later a grim-faced Chris walked out to the porch where Alex was seated in the rocking chair.

"Alex, Dena's on the phone. Says it's pretty urgent."

She pushed herself out of her chair and ran into the house. She grabbed the phone just inside the hallway.

"Dena, what's happened?" she demanded.

"You were right." Her quiet voice throbbed. "There was a rape in the parking lot last night. It was the same man you caught before. Luckily one of the security guards happened to come by before it could have gotten much worse." She couldn't go on.

Alex swore fiercely under her breath. "Who was it?" she asked tightly.

"Caryn Warren."

She closed her eyes and recalled the petite blond woman, who, ironically, worked as Walt St. Clair's secretary. "Did St. Clair say anything about security when he heard about this?"

"He mentioned that it was a good thing the guard came along when he did. They did catch the man."

Alex took deep breaths to control her temper, but it wasn't helping much. "See if you can get a copy of the police report for me. That guy isn't getting out this time if I have anything to say about it. I also want you to find me a voodoo doll that looks like St. Clair and a lot of pins. I want enough to make him damn uncomfortable for a long time," she finished on a savage note.

A few moments later she slammed the phone down and reached up to rake her fingers through her hair.

"Did you kill it?"

Alex spun around, ready to fight, and Jared was the perfect victim. "There was another attack in the parking garage last night," she began hotly.

"Who?" he demanded tersely.

"Caryn Warren." She laughed harshly. "Ironic, isn't it? Well, I've had it, really had it this time and now my suggestions are ultimatums. I want those cameras installed *today.*"

"All right," he agreed quietly without hesitation.

By now she was past anger. Her body was shaking with an inner rage. Her eyes burned with tears that refused to fall.

"Damn it, Jared, did it have to be rape to bring you to your senses?" she rasped, uncaring that Rashid stood behind him and was listening to every word. "This could have been prevented from the beginning if you hadn't listened to that pompous ass, St. Clair." She spun around and walked to the open front door.

"Where are you going?" Jared's voice lashed out with the strength of a whip snapping overhead.

"You can get along with just Rashid's men today. Right now I don't think I could give you the protection you pay me for." The front door slammed shut after her.

"She's wrong, you know." Rashid's quiet voice broke the charged silence.

"About what?" Jared asked, inwardly wanting nothing more than to strangle her.

"Instinctively, she would protect you. She is someone who would give her life for you, and not because she is well paid for it either." He laid a hand on Jared's shoulder. "We can dispense with our talks today. I'm sure you have other matters to attend to. If I could make use of one of your men to drive me into Santa Barbara?"

"Of course." His mind was clearly somewhere else.

Needing to get away from the house, Alex ran down to the barn and saddled a horse. Despite Tim's warnings when he could see how agitated she was, she rode out.

She lost track of time as she gave the mare her head. She had no particular direction in mind. She just wanted time to herself.

When she found a narrow stream she reined in her horse and dismounted. She settled herself on a bed of dead leaves and stared up at the mountains.

"You're not too bright, are you?"

Alex slowly turned her head and found an angry Jared looking down at her. He dismounted and walked over to her.

"Do you realize how long you've been gone?" he snarled.

She looked around and finally noticed the deepening shadows that heralded dusk. "No, but I'm sure you'll tell me," she replied indifferently. She started when something was tossed into her lap.

"Mavis was afraid you might be hungry," he explained. "Personally . . ."

"As far as you were concerned, I could starve?" she finished on a sardonic note, opening the paper bag to find a thick roast beef sandwich and a small thermos of coffee.

Jared squatted down on his heels and watched her hungrily demolish the sandwich.

"The cameras will be installed by tomorrow," he said quietly. "I had a long talk with Dena too."

"Oh?"

"She told me about your budget meeting with Walt."

"Really?"

Jared's features hardened at the monosyllables he was receiving. "Why didn't you tell me about the trouble he was giving you?"

Alex finished the last of her sandwich and faced him with cold eyes. "It was my problem and I preferred to handle it my way," she said stubbornly.

"And because you refused to tell me, you lost."

"I wouldn't have if this hadn't come up," she argued.

Jared reached out and gripped her wrist, always marveling how much power was in the delicate bone structure. "You make me so damn mad!" he gritted.

"Welcome to the club!" Alex snatched her hand away as if his touch burned her and scrambled to her feet. A moment later she was on her horse urging her back to the house.

Alex was conscious of Jared following her every step of the way back to the barn. Her imagination even told her that it was his warm breath on her nape instead of the cold wind blowing around her.

When she reached the barn, only her sense of responsibility forced her to stay and unsaddle her horse.

A steel viselike hand grabbed her shoulder and wrenched her around. "You sure picked the right way to try to break your neck." Jared's eyes shot sparks. As he stared down at her mutinous features, something else took over. "Damn you," he groaned before his mouth closed over hers.

Jared's other hand clasped her neck, pulling her head back as far as it would go. His body had pressed her back until they were molded perfectly together against one of the stalls.

Alex's own arms slid around his waist and pressed her palms flat against the slight curve of his buttocks.

"Jared." Her whisper was lost among the rough possession of his tongue. She could feel his hardening length against her pliant softness.

In reply, he moved his hips suggestively against hers. His hands had unbuttoned her shirt and torn apart the fragile, lacy bra so that his lips could drift down to cover the pulsing coral-tipped nipple. Alex cried out, feeling the pull of his lips all the way down to the center of her body. Her hands were equally busy sliding under the rough denim of his jeans even as her sane half spoke out loud.

"Someone could come in," she gasped as Jared's teeth bit down gently on the nipple, then pulled on the sensitized skin.

"Tim drove Rashid into Santa Barbara," he rasped. "I can't wait for you, Alex, not anymore."

Alex was in a daze as Jared took her hand and pulled her down the length of the barn to a ladder then pushed her up it. When she reached the top, she stumbled until his hands steadied her and spun her around to fall against him.

"This is crazy." She took deep breaths but only inhaled the musky scent of his skin mixed with the earthier fragrance of horseflesh and perspiration.

"No crazier than we'd be if we tried to walk away from each other right now," he informed her in a rough voice.

Jared swiftly unbuttoned his shirt and dropped it on the hay. Alex's shirt soon followed. He pulled back slightly to feast his eyes on her rapidly heaving breasts. The dark, blazing lights in the green orbs sent a tightening ache throughout her body and tautened the nipples until they stood out, silently begging for his touch.

"I want to see all of you, Alex." Jared's voice was husky with passion.

This was no time to think coherently, only to act. There was no modesty or coyness in her movements as her hands dropped to her belt buckle. A moment later her jeans and boots were discarded. Now wearing only a pair of delicate lace bikini panties, she faced him.

"Your turn," she prompted softly.

Jared's slow smile was seduction in itself. "I've always fantasized about stripping for a woman," he murmured, his hands dropping to the waistband of his jeans. He took his time in unsnapping and unzipping, as if knowing the anticipation was most pleasurable. It took him a moment to pull off his boots and socks, then it was back up to push the denims down his legs and step out of them, sliding them to one side with his foot. He pushed his hands inside the dark blue briefs and just as slowly pushed them down over muscular thighs and strong legs leading to the equally muscular calves. Alex couldn't keep her eyes from the vitally masculine figure before her. If Jared had fantasized about stripping for a woman, then her inner fantasy must have been to watch a man strip just for her. A private showing for one. And what a showing! She knew that his body was in excellent physical shape. The few times she had seen him at the swimming pool told her that. His broad chest was tanned an even bronze with the curling hairs accenting his flat nipples then arrowing down to his potent masculinity. Her body was essentially female, complementing his definitely male contours. Not only complementing, but reacting to his maleness. She could feel the warmth rush through her body at the arousing thoughts of his lovemaking. Her nipples peaked, not from the cool air, but from the idea of his caressing them, and she could feel the steady throb in her lower body silently calling out for him to fill her with his strength. This was no fantasy, but a reality worth holding on to for all time.

When Jared next took Alex into his arms, an explosion erupted. This was no time for gentle caresses or for learning about each other. The sheer sexual tension that had built up between them for the past six months fulminated now in ecstasy. He dropped to his knees and pulled her down with him. Jared lay back, drawing Alex over his body and fitting her to every male angle. Her fingertips eagerly explored his chest, her lips following the lust-arousing path. With eyes closed he tipped his head back, groaning when her teeth nibbled his tiny nipples until they stood at attention, mimicking hers. Unable to take anymore, his hands grasped the curve of her buttocks to hold her to him as he rolled over to imprison her under him and to fill her with his driving heat.

They were caught up in the fiery sensations until they could only be considered a part of each other. One couldn't breathe without the other; they were caught up in a glittering world neither had known existed. When Alex felt she couldn't go on, she moaned Jared's name and sunk her teeth into his shoulder. Her last coherent thought was hearing him breathe her name when his body stiffened to join hers in a torrent of desire.

Alex was gradually aware of the air chilling her body where the pressure of Jared's wasn't warming it. Faint tremors were still running through her because his hand was idly stroking the curve of her bare hip and thigh.

"About all I have the energy to say is 'wow,' " Jared murmured, his eyes filled with warmth for the woman beside him.

She pressed her lips against the tiny indentations her

teeth had left in his shoulder. "Tired you out, did I?" she teased.

"I sure didn't expect a volcano hidden deep inside that sexy body of yours." His own lips wandered over her forehead, tasting the faint salt on the damp skin. A nagging thought persisted in Jared's mind, wondering how many other men had tasted the white-hot passion Alex had just displayed. He couldn't deny the other women in his life, but for some selfish reason, he wanted only her passion to be given to him.

"I certainly didn't expect to be made love to in a smelly old hayloft, a roll in the hay so to speak," she snickered softly, her gentle laughter proclaiming the play on words.

"A roll in the hay!" Jared pretended to be offended. "I'll have you know this took a lot of planning, lady. Do you realize how difficult it is to get reservations for this place?"

She turned, slightly curving her body against his. "No wonder, these mattresses are as hard as boards." Her forefinger traced a random pattern over his chest, circling each nipple, then spiraling down to his navel. She twisted suddenly and dropped a moist kiss in the center of it, drawing a sharp breath from Jared. "Got to you, didn't I?" she teased, looking up.

Jared reached down and pulled her on top of him. "You got to me in more ways than one," he said thickly, cradling his hand behind her head and drawing her down for his kiss that deepened as soon as it began. He knew no woman had ever tasted like her, felt like her, or moved against him like her. Alex gave as good as she got, which only sent Jared further into oblivion. "When was the last time a man made you feel like this, Alex?" he punished himself by asking. "When was the last time you sent a man to heaven and hell at the same moment?"

The moment was gone. Alex's eyes clouded over at his question, not seeing the difficulty it took for him to ask.

She sat up and groped around for her shirt and jeans. "Damn you for ruining this," she snarled, picking up the shirt and starting to pull it on only to find it was Jared's. She threw it from her and found the right one this time.

"Oh, no." He sat up and reached for her. "A few minutes ago you were purring like a kitten, no more wildcat around me, Alex. I know better now."

"Know what?"

His smile was boyish and endearing. "That deep down you have a wild and passionate nature," he confided in a mock whisper. "A regular wanton woman."

Alex didn't want to smile at his words, but she couldn't help it. "You're incorrigible."

"Just sex-crazed." His eyes darkened with remembered passion. "I want you again, Alex," he said roughly.

She didn't want to reveal how badly she also wanted him. "Isn't lovemaking in the barn just a bit adolescent?" She picked up his shirt and threw it playfully at his face. "My God, this is something straight out of high school!"

Jared stood up and winced when a few of his muscles protested after the hard floor of the loft. "I guess there wasn't enough hay for our mattress." He groped around for his socks, but could find only one. "You're right; I am too old for this."

Alex finger-combed the tangles and wisps of hay from her hair. "If Mavis sees us like this, she'll know for sure what we've been doing up here."

"Then the best thing for us to do is to continue with our adolescent ways and sneak in the back way." Jared was busy pulling on his jeans.

A few minutes later Alex followed Jared out of the barn and around to the side of the house near her bedroom.

"What are you planning to do, push me through my bedroom window?" she asked him when they reached the end of the wing.

He shook his head. "Something much better." He led her to a sliding glass door and inserted a key into the lock and opened it.

Once inside, Jared reached over and tapped a wall switch, bringing the room to light. Alex blinked her eyes to adjust to the brightness and looked around with interest.

A good part of one wall was taken up by a stone fireplace and another revealed a king-size platform bed with a cinnamon and gold striped quilt on top. A nearby bookcase was filled to capacity with volumes on many subjects.

"This is your room?"

"A brilliant piece of detective work." A smile curved his mouth.

Alex shook her head, finally realizing a lot of things. "No wonder you heard me cry out that night," she mused. "You're only a couple of doors away from me, right?"

"Right."

Alex shook her head in silent wonder. She had allowed Jared to make love to her, and for all intents and purposes, by remaining here in his room invited his lovemaking again. At that moment she wasn't sure what to say. What did one say to the man who was not only her employer, but the man who just made love to her?

"I guess I can find my room easily enough from here," she said casually, turning toward the door.

Jared swiftly crossed the room and slid his arms around her. "The bed here is more than large enough for two people," he coaxed silkily, angling one warm hand under her shirt.

The fires which had been smoking embers moments before were rapidly stoked back to flames by his touch. Alex couldn't comprehend how this could happen so quickly. Where was the casual employer/employee relationship they had shared? She licked her suddenly dry lips.

"You're not playing fair, Jared," she said huskily, wishing the moist tip of his tongue wouldn't send shock waves throughout her body.

"You're right." He seemed to be fascinated with the shape and taste of her ear.

Alex tried to swallow and even found that a chore. Her fingers rested on his crossed arms but made no move to disengage his grip. She could feel the mounting heat flowing through her veins. For one insane, crazy moment she wanted to turn around and tear his clothes from his body so that he could drive her insensible the way he had in the barn.

"Umm, sounds like a great idea to me." He apparently had read her thoughts.

"You're a dirty old man, Mr. Templeton." Her voice was hoarse and filled with mixed emotions.

"That's because you have the kind of body a dirty old man craves, Mrs. Page," he chuckled, turning her around in his arms. When his mouth fastened on hers, there was no coherent thought. As before, they silently communicated with lips, teeth, tongues, and hands.

Alex's clothes were swept from her as she was lowered onto the cool sheets of Jared's bed. She arched up to meet his warmth as his hand teased her inner thigh, seeking all her secrets. Again there was a passionate outburst between them. Jared's thrusting body matched Alex's pulsing form perfectly. She clung to him, afraid that losing hold she would lose hold of herself. Now she knew what it felt like to be in the middle of an explosion. An explosion Jared shared with her as his body sent her over the edge only to follow her in the descent.

Afterward Alex lay limply in Jared's arms and took deep breaths to slow her racing pulse. Her heart beat so rapidly, she was afraid it would leave her body. Her only consolation was that his heartbeats weren't any slower.

"No gentle loving for us, Alex." Jared's husky voice warmed her cheek. "Only two people like us could create what we shared tonight . . . something rare and beautiful."

She suddenly felt a fear of being mentally submerged by this man. She was strong-minded, but he was much stronger than she. Could she resist?

She pressed her cheek against the damp hairs on his chest. "It's also dangerous." Jared had to strain to hear her low voice.

His hands idly roamed the smooth skin of her back. "Afraid I'll have a heart attack during the throes of passion?" He seemed to find this notion amusing.

She shook her head. "Not you. I have a hunch you'll still be going strong when you're eighty." The events of the day and the tumultuous evening were catching up with her and she was finding it difficult to keep her eyes open.

Jared's hand now rested against her nape, massaging away the last of her tension.

"Umm, nice," Alex mumbled, curling her body around his.

Jared remained awake after she had fallen into a deep, relaxed sleep. "Yes, very nice" was his murmur before he joined her in sleep.

Alex smiled sleepily, enjoying the secure warmth of her electric blanket. She snuggled farther under the covers, then stiffened. The heat she was enjoying wasn't from her electric blanket, but from an entirely different source.

"Good morning."

She kept her eyes closed and groaned softly. "Tell me this is a bad dream," she pleaded with the male voice.

"It's not."

"A hangover?" she ventured hopefully, then gasped as a warm hand moved over her rib cage and down her abdomen to her thighs.

"Wrong again." Jared rolled over on top of her and trapped her legs under one of his. "Shall we work on a cure?"

She was fighting the treacherous flames licking her nerve endings from the intimate caress of his probing fingers. "Please." Her soft-voiced plea was echoed in her eyes, but what was she pleading for?

His lips traced a flaming path along her jawline. "I'd be honored to," he murmured against her skin.

Her hands lifted and placed themselves against his chest. "Jared, I have to go take a shower before breakfast," she protested while her body screamed out for his possession.

"Great idea; you scrub my back and I'll scrub yours." His eyes twinkled wickedly.

"No, thanks." With a bit of effort, she pushed him away and jumped out of bed. She reached for her clothes and began pulling them on.

Jared lay back to enjoy the show, his arms crossed behind his head. "There's no reason why you can't move your things in here now."

Alex's fingers froze in their chore of buttoning her shirt. His meaning was all too clear. She slowly turned around and shook her head. "No, Jared," she said gently. "When I walk out of here, I'll still be Alex and you'll still be Mr. Templeton. That's the way it has to be." She tucked her shirt into her jeans and walked over to the bed. A light kiss was pressed against his lips and she moved away before he could try to deepen it.

"You mean that, don't you?" His voice was tinged with disbelief. Women clamored for the chance to share Jared Templeton's bed. They didn't calmly walk away from him as Alex was just doing. Anger and dented male ego entered the conversation. "So all I was good for was a quick roll in the hay. Those were your words, not mine," he said sarcastically.

Alex showed none of the hurt she felt at his words. "Don't worry, Jared—" her low voice was laced with faint mockery—"you'll survive. You always have." When she reached the door, she said over her shoulder as casually as if they were an old married couple, "See you at breakfast."

Left alone, Jared frowned, annoyed that Alex could so easily leave him. This was something new for him. He was usually the one in a hurry to leave while the woman wanted nothing more than to snuggle up to him or, worse, talk. Funny, he never had a desire to just lay in bed and cuddle up the way he wanted to with Alex this morning. She may be his bodyguard, but she certainly aroused some protective instincts in him, if not some of the more basic ones! For the first time, Jared found himself wanting to relax with a woman in his arms and enjoy more than early morning lovemaking. He wanted to share a quiet breakfast with her, talk with her, and just be with her. He drew a deep breath and sat up, pushing the covers aside. After what happened between them last night, he sincerely doubted that it would be the only time Alex would share his bed. They were too much of a matched pair to be apart for long.

Once Alex reached her room, she could do nothing more than collapse wearily on her bed. She couldn't remember ever feeling so drained. The most passionate lovemaking with Dennis paled in comparison with the hours spent in Jared's arms. It was as if he took her energy from her and gave it back only to take it from her again. Her body tightened in reaction to her thoughts. Refusing to give in, she pushed herself off the bed and headed for the bathroom for a quick shower.

Chris shot her several puzzled glances when she appeared for breakfast. Jared had reverted to the congenial host, treating Alex with courtesy and not as the sensual lover of the night before. Rashid wished her a polite good morning, then turned to Jared to ask him several questions. It was as if the outburst of the day before hadn't happened.

Alex was grateful to spend the morning outside instead of in Jared's study. She didn't think she could spend the next few hours in a businesslike atmosphere while memories of the previous night intruded, and they would certainly intrude. She was positive Jared would make sure of that.

Mavis brought out a tray holding a coffee server and a plate of freshly baked sugar cookies. Alex thanked the housekeeper and bit into the chewy cookie. Guard duty had never been so easy.

As the days passed, Jared still maintained a respectful distance, much to Alex's confusion. She spent a lot of sleepless nights recalling the time spent in the barn and later in Jared's bedroom. At first a strange panic overtook her, insisting that it was her fault he hadn't come near her again. At the same time, she reminded herself that was what she wanted and he was only respecting her wishes. Except Alex now found the nights long and solitary.

Jared had kept his promise. The security cameras had been installed. Alex's revised budget would receive a fair review by Walt St. Clair when she returned to L.A. All of this was relayed to her through Chris.

"I think you got off easy," he confided to her one morning.

"Oh?"

"Anyone else who dared to scream at the boss the way you did would turn up in Outer Mongolia. Instead, for once, *he* followed orders. That's why I say you're a very lucky lady."

Alex smiled wryly at his words. Was she all that lucky? She was beginning to wonder. Or had she paid for Jared's promise in the form of one night spent in his bed? She had always been very careful to keep her life in tidy little compartments. In the space of a few hours those compartments had been thrown into a jumble. She was looking forward to the day when she could return to L.A. and resume her life.

The surprising part was that not once had she considered giving up her job. No, she had run away once before when she left the navy. This time she wouldn't run away. She'd stay and prove to Jared that night was nothing more than a casual coupling and she would continue to think that until she began to believe her own untruths.

One Monday afternoon Alex sat in the study unaware that Jared was studying her profile outlined in the pale winter light. She had been so lost in her own thoughts that it took a while to realize that Jared was laughing and getting up to shake a smiling Rashid's hand. It then took her a few moments longer to understand that Jared and Rashid had finally agreed on a price for the oil wells in question.

"We must celebrate this evening," Rashid announced, smiling brightly at Alex. "At Jared's expense, of course, since I am allowing him to pay me such a paltry sum for my wells."

"Paltry?" His eyebrows rose. "That 'paltry sum' is going to upset my accounting department a great deal."

Rashid continued smiling as he walked over to Alex and lifted her hand to his lips. "You only fared so well, my friend, because I could not truly concentrate on business when I was able to feast my eyes on this beautiful lady," he informed Jared all the while keeping his eyes on Alex's face.

She laughed at his elaborate flattery but stopped when she saw Jared's features darkening with what looked like anger. What could have gotten him so upset?

"I know just the place to celebrate." Rashid turned to Jared. "That charming restaurant overlooking the water at Stearns Wharf. I'm sure Madame Page will enjoy it."

"Perhaps, but I won't be required to accompany you, Mr. Kalim, now that the negotiations are over," she said quietly.

"Yes, you will," Jared snapped. "Be ready at six." He turned away and strode out of the room.

With a thoughtful frown marring his handsome face, Rashid watched Jared's leavetaking. "As you would say, Jared seems to be bent out of shape," he commented.

"No," Alex softly contradicted him. "Mr. Templeton never loses his perspective." She preferred to forget the night when he had appeared past all coherent thought.

Having packed little in the way of dressy clothing, Alex didn't have any problem in deciding what to wear.

After a leisurely bubble bath, she smoothed scented body lotion on her skin and washed her hair, then twisted it up into a smooth coil on top of her head.

She slipped on dark purple silk pants and a matching kimono-style jacket with a pale lilac camisole underneath. Dressy while remaining typically California casual.

Jared had also dressed expensively casual in tailored dark gray slacks and a pale gray shirt left open at the throat.

At the restaurant they were ushered to a side dining room that catered to a more elite clientele. With Chris making a fourth in their party, Alex was seated next to him with Jared seated directly across from her and Rashid on his right.

After the waiter had taken their orders for drinks, Jared asked Chris to explain a few technical matters to Rashid.

Alex listened to the conversation with half an ear while glancing out the window to the dark water lighted by the pleasure craft moored in the harbor and by the streetlamps on the wharf. Feeling an uneasy prickling sensation along her nape, she slowly turned her head to encounter Jared's smoldering eyes.

Her breath caught in her throat as she saw the direction of his gaze. It was centered on the rounded curve of her breasts, which immediately swelled under his assessing glance. His mental caress slid up to the clean lines of her throat, then moved up to her mouth and remained there. Alex resisted the urge to slide her tongue over her lips, sensing it would be construed as a provocative gesture under the seductive gaze. The silent communication was more potent than words.

When the waiter returned with their drinks, Alex gratefully accepted her Scotch and water. When she lifted the glass to her lips, Jared continued to watch her actions, and his lazy study of her movements continued throughout the meal.

With each bite of her lobster, his eyes watched the fork rise to her mouth and taste the succulent meat. Alex found it difficult to concentrate on her food with her silent sentinel. When she lifted her wineglass, he did likewise. The expression in his eyes was dark and mysterious, but she felt as if he were silently telling her their moves were perfectly matched, the way their bodies matched in a primitive rhythm. With his eyes, his actions, his thoughts, Jared was making love to Alex. He couldn't have affected her any more deeply than if he had physically touched her. She was never more relieved than when the meal was finished.

During the drive back to the ranch Alex sat in the back

seat with Chris and carried on a quiet conversation. It didn't help that each time she looked up she would see Jared's eyes staring in the rearview mirror and watching her. She longed to know why he was doing this to her, but she wasn't sure if she would like his answer.

When they reached the house later that evening Alex quietly bade the men a good night and headed for her room.

She had just placed her hand on the doorknob when her name was softly called out. Turning around, she wasn't surprised to see Jared standing behind her. Smiling crookedly, he leaned over and placed a hand on either side of her to prevent escape.

"You knew what to wear tonight, didn't you?" His warm breath, scented with brandy and the cheroots he smoked, wafted over her face. "Something that would drive me out of my mind."

"Did I?" she asked without coyness.

"Sure, you did." His lips were alarmingly close to the corner of one eye. "You knew those pants would lovingly hug that curved derriere of yours and that nothing of a top just barely covers your breasts while screaming to the world you're not wearing a bra." One hand moved down to lightly rest on the curve of her hip, kneading the slick material. "Hmm, French bikini panties too. Quite a potent combination." The tip of his tongue teased the corner of her eye.

Alex closed her eyes under the moist tip trailing her skin. Her breath was coming faster and she could feel her skin warming under the caress.

"You feel it, too, don't you, Alex?" Jared whispered, a strange intensity in his voice.

"I feel nothing," she lied.

He took her hand and placed it just inside his shirt. The uneven thud of his heart was strongly echoing her own rapid pulse. He moved even closer to her until the lower part of his body was molded to hers. She shivered at the feel of his arousal, knowing she was the cause.

"Purely a physical reaction," she said huskily.

Jared's teeth flashed white in the darkness. His hand moved from her hip to her breast, easily tracing the turgid nipple. "Like this?" He bent his head and circled the silk-covered tip with his tongue. Alex shut her eyes, barely able to suppress the moan that started in the depths of her throat, but Jared heard enough to know she was deeply affected. He now transferred his attention to the other nipple. Swallowing a gasp, Alex's hands tugged at his hair and pulled his head up to hers. Her parted lips with the tip of her tongue at its center was the only invitation he needed.

His hands slid around her back to keep her tightly against him. There was an urgent hunger to his kiss, as if he couldn't get enough of her. His tongue curled around hers, inviting her love play. He wanted to absorb all of her—her taste, her scent, the feel of her. Alex was a willing participant undulating her hips against him in sensual invitation.

Suddenly Jared dragged his mouth away and rested his damp forehead against hers. For a moment all that could be heard was the sound of his ragged breathing in unison with hers.

"Good night, Alex," he finally said. He straightened up, released her, and began to turn away.

She looked up with dazed eyes at this sudden turn of events.

"We'll be flying out of here at ten," he said in a more normal voice. "I trust you'll be ready by then."

A bitter smile touched her lips, although her insides were tied up in fierce knots. "Don't worry, Mr. Templeton." Her voice dripped icicles. "I'll be more than ready to leave here." She spun around, entered the bathroom, and closed the door firmly behind her.

Even a cold shower couldn't banish the pain racking her body. When she finally went to bed, it was a long time before she drifted into a restless sleep, then only to awaken at dawn with a fierce headache. After that, she lay in bed, feeling a new kind of ache take over her body.

Alex awoke later in the morning feeling as if a tank had driven over her. A brief trip to the bathroom and an even briefer look at her pale features in the mirror was enough to send her back to bed. She had no appetite for breakfast.

She was still in bed when an abrupt knock sounded at her door, then flung open without waiting for an invitation to enter.

"Don't tell me you overslept?" Jared demanded, moving over to stand by the bed.

"Go away," Alex groaned, not having the strength even to turn her head to look at him.

Jared's face creased in a frown as he looked down at her. He bent over and carefully cupped her face with his hands to turn her toward him. The heat radiating from her skin was unmistakable.

"You're sick," he exclaimed.

"No kidding," she croaked, lifting a weak hand to brush him away. "Don't worry, I'll be up in time to leave. I just don't want any breakfast."

"You're not going anywhere." His hands felt cool against her face and forehead. He straightened up and walked into the bathroom. The sound of running water could be heard, then it stopped. A moment later Alex could feel a cool, damp cloth bathing her face. "Feel better?" he asked softly.

"Yes," she whispered.

"Do you have any pain?"

"Just in every bone in my body," Alex admitted wearily. "I'm thirty-two years old and I'm falling apart already. I guess my warranty ran out. Please don't tell Chris. He's been predicting my downfall for the past year."

A faint smile flickered across Jared's face. "If you can retain your sense of humor, you're doing all right. I guarantee the last thing happening to you is your falling apart."

"Please, just go away and let me die in peace," she begged.

"Don't get any ideas of leaving that bed," he ordered, walking toward the door. "I'll send Mavis in with some juice. You're to stay there until I say otherwise." The door closed quietly behind him.

Alex didn't find it difficult to obey Jared's command. At that moment she doubted if she could find the energy to move her big toe. She was just dozing off when Mavis bustled in carrying a tray.

"Hmm, you do look peaked," the housekeeper commented, placing the tray on the night table before assisting Alex into a half-sitting position. "I brought you juice and a soft-boiled egg."

"I have to get dressed," Alex protested faintly. "We're leaving this morning. I'm not even packed yet."

"Child, you're not going anywhere," Mavis said firmly, now busy straightening the tumbled covers. "Jared said you're to stay in bed until you're better and that's just what you're going to do. You don't need to fret, everyone's already gone, so you'll have plenty of peace and quiet."

"Gone?" Alex gave a dismayed gasp. "Everyone?"

"Left a half hour ago. Jared said he'd tell your secretary you're ill and that you're not to worry about anything. I'll be back in a little while and I expect to see that you've eaten." She was out the door.

Alex lay back, allowing the numbness to wash over her body. Jared hadn't even come in to say good-bye. No matter what, she could have hoped he would at least have had the courtesy to do that. Obviously not. She had no appetite for her breakfast, but out of deference to Mavis, she ate.

By the time the housekeeper returned for the tray, Alex had dozed off, feeling very alone and unwanted.

She spent most of the day sleeping or just staring up at the ceiling. Mavis brought her a mug of soup for lunch, but she could sip only about half of it before pushing the tray away. She blamed her lack of interest in food more on her illness than the fact that Jared had left without saying good-bye to her.

When it turned dark, Mavis came in to turn on a light and see if Alex wanted anything. She had made sure to keep Alex supplied with juices and a pitcher of ice water all day. The last time she had gone in, Alex had been sound asleep, so she only turned the lamp on at its dimmest setting.

Alex wasn't sure what later awoke her, only that something or someone was in her room. Stirring, she turned her head to see a tall figure standing with his back to her near the window.

"Jared?" she called out softly, unable to believe her eyes.

The figure turned and walked over to her bedside. "How are you feeling?" He leaned over and braced one hand against the top of the headboard.

"But you went to L.A. this morning." She still thought she was dreaming that he was standing there.

"Just to check in, sign whatever needed to be signed, and let the board know I'm still breathing," he joked.

Alex's smile was a faint semblance of her usual one. "Meaning you went down there and rattled some cages."

"Just have to show them I'm still the boss." Jared's fingers trailed lightly across her cheek and down her jawline. "Mavis gave me strict orders that I wasn't to overtire you, but I did want to see how you were feeling." He sat down on the edge of the bed where Alex had slid over to clear a space for him.

She wasn't sure if it was Jared's touch or her elevated temperature that was giving her the hot flashes. "Don't you have to go back to your office?" She knew he rarely took any time off for himself and this length of time away from the business was a record for him.

"Trying to get rid of me already?" He lifted a teasing eyebrow while sending his hand drifting along the neckline of her nightgown and down over the soft roundness of her breast, noting the nipple standing up at his brief, teasing touch.

She shook her head. "It's just not something you normally do," she whispered, wishing her breathing hadn't sped up at the sensual caress.

Jared lightly brushed stray strands of hair away from her forehead and framed her flushed features with his cupped palms. "There's a lot of things I don't normally do," he replied cryptically, looking down at her with an intense gaze.

Alex studied him, not knowing that her pale features only intensified her delicate bone structure. "Why did you come back?" she couldn't resist asking, reaching up to fiddle with one of his shirt buttons and slowly unfastening it to reveal the crisp hairs.

His smile was enigmatic. "Because it's nice to be around you when you're so pliable," he murmured, bending over to brush a gentle, mind-shattering kiss against her lips. For a scant moment his tongue appeared, tracing the outline and leaving his mark before parting her soft lips and tasting the sweet, dark caverns of her mouth. Alex moaned softly and slid her arms around his neck, but as she raised her head a weak dizziness overcame her, a reminder of her illness. She gasped and dropped back down onto her pillow. Jared smiled ruefully. "For a moment I forgot how sick you are," he said, caressing her cheek. He stood up and turned to walk out the door. "Mavis said she'll be bringing you some soup and that you're to drink it all. I'll come see you first thing in the morning. If you need anything during the night, just call out. I'll leave my door open."

After Jared left, Alex lay there, unable to believe that he had flown back up because of her. Again the question came to her, but why? She had a deep-seated feeling that she'd soon find out.

CHAPTER SIX

Alex didn't recover as quickly as she anticipated. Months of meals on the run, when she did think to eat, and nights of little sleep had left her with little resistance to the virus that attacked her.

Jared had become so alarmed when Alex's temperature rose to a dangerous level on the second day, he insisted a doctor come out to treat her. He was not happy when the doctor explained that the cause of her illness was due to her lack of taking care of herself.

It was a little over a week before she began to feel a bit better. She crawled out of bed one afternoon and made her way to the bathroom.

"Ooh," she groaned, studying her reflection in the mirror. Where her skin had always portrayed a sheer, translucent finish, it was now a pasty white. Usually clear bright-green eyes appeared to have a cloudy film over them, and her usually shiny hair hung in limp strands, having been without a shampoo for the past week.

"Not your usual glamorous self, are you?"

Alex slowly turned her head to see Jared leaning against the doorway.

"Yes, thank you, I'm feeling much better," she mocked in a husky voice. "Just because I look as if I belong in one of Edgar Allan Poe's poems doesn't mean I don't have any feelings." She braced her hands against the cool porcelain sink, feeling her small reserve of strength rapidly leave her body.

Jared took immediate notice and stepped forward to take her into his arms. "You just have to play the tough guy, don't you?" he asked gruffly, shaking his head in wonder at her stubborn nature.

"You've got it," Alex muttered, resting her head against his shoulder. "Never say die, that's me."

He placed her back in bed and pulled the covers around her. He took his time in adjusting the blanket over her breasts.

"Will you stop it!" She irritably slapped at his wandering hands. "Have some pity for a dying woman."

"You should be so lucky." He smiled as he sat on the edge of the bed. His eyes betrayed his concern for the dark hollows of her cheeks and the unnatural pallor of her skin. "After a good dose of Mavis's cooking and some fresh country air you'll soon be back to your old cynical self."

"I plan to be back in my office the day after tomorrow," Alex argued.

"No way."

"I have a budget meeting to prepare for."

"Nope."

"You're due to fly to London next week and I'm supposed to tag along."

"Canceled."

Alex studied Jared through narrowed eyes. It wasn't difficult to see that any of her objections would be overruled. "I hate being sick," she stated flatly.

"Good, because you're not exactly the model patient." He leaned over and dropped a kiss on her forehead. "You look as if you're ready for a nap."

"I just woke up from one," she pointed out irritably.

"You need to build up your strength," Jared said softly, rising to his feet. "Take advantage of all this coddling, Alex. I have an idea this is something new for you."

She couldn't argue that her eyelids were drooping. She hated this helpless feeling of being out of control.

"You just wait until I'm back on my feet." Her words were slurring.

Jared smiled again, a gentle smile that Alex didn't see. "Baby, that's just what I'm waiting for."

It turned out to be another three days before Alex could get out of bed and stay out for any length of time. As it was, she was allowed only as far as the living room, where she was ensconced on the couch in a bundle of blankets with books and magazines placed at a convenient distance.

She was surprised at the time Jared was spending away from his office. Although his mornings were spent in his study on the telephone to Chris, he spent a good part of the afternoons and evenings with her.

On one such afternoon Alex finally decided to question him.

"Jared, are you sure you should spend so much time away from your work?" she asked casually. "After all, there's so much going on right now between the deal you made with Rashid and the dealings with those London bankers."

She wasn't surprised when he took his time answering. By going to the bar and fixing himself a drink he delayed his reply even more.

"Maybe I'm trying to find out how well they can do without me there," he said lightly.

Alex shook her head. "Not you. You have to be in control. You need to know everything that's going on, to be in on it all."

Jared walked over to the couch and perched himself on the arm. "What has it gotten me?" There was a strange intensity in his voice. "I head one of the 'five hundred' corporations, but I have little to call my own. I'm sure I'm considered one of the playboys of the business world, but I haven't found enough time even to properly court a woman, if I had found one who suited me. What woman would have put up with my erratic schedules or preoccupation with my work? I certainly wouldn't blame any woman who would accuse my career of being my mistress and, believe me, I've heard many complaints about that when I've had to beg off from a social engagement because of something that had come up at the office. Chris is nursing an ulcer because of our hectic schedule. You've been sick because of that same schedule." He uttered a harsh laugh that was sad in its own way. "Do you know what the newspapers call us? The Dynamic Trio; the three people no one can stop. It makes you stop and wonder if it's all worthwhile. What will we have to show for it besides making Fernwood even larger and more powerful? Who will we leave it to?" he asked bleakly.

Alex reached out and grasped his clenched hand with her own. She was gaining a lot of knowledge into the inner man that astounded her. In a blinding flash she caught a glimpse of a very lonely man. A man who for all his riches and choice of beautiful women to grace his side and bed still spent a great deal of time alone. With an instinct as old as time itself, she rested her cheek against their clasped hands.

"Why do you do this?" she whispered, still fighting the softer emotions coursing through her veins. "I swear you're only trying to make me feel sorry for you so I won't ask for a raise."

Lean, slightly callused fingers stroked her cheek, then a pair of warm lips followed the same path. "Shall I tell you what you do to me?" he murmured in return. "Or show you?" The fingers pressed lightly against her lips before she could reply. "No protests now, Alex. Our time is coming."

Later that night she lay awake pondering his words. Her emotional side wished for a repeat of that tumultuous night with Jared while her rational half told her it would be disastrous. She knew she couldn't be his lover and his protector too. Tim was right, who was going to protect her?

The next day Alex felt strong enough to get up and dress for breakfast. Jared's surprised look and smile when she walked into the dining room was enough of a good morning for her.

"Looks like you lost about a size." He glanced at her jeans with a critical eye.

"Don't keep it in, Jared," she advised sardonically. "Go ahead, say what you feel."

"She's definitely feeling better," Mavis announced, walking in and placing a full plate in front of Jared.

"Does that mean I can have more than a soft-boiled egg and oatmeal?" Alex wrinkled her nose at the memory of the unappetizing fare.

"Maybe a couple of pieces of bacon," the housekeeper compromised, before bustling back to the kitchen.

"She thinks a lot of you," Jared told Alex when they had been left alone.

"I like her too." She smiled. "I have to admit it's nice sometimes to have someone fuss over you."

"If you feel like it, we can go for a short ride after breakfast. It isn't too cold out today," he suggested.

Alex's face brightened at the idea. She had to admit she was beginning to feel cooped up lately.

As promised, after breakfast Jared took Alex on a short ride into the hills. Her eyes began to regain their glow of happiness at being outdoors and enjoying the fresh air.

"Isn't it beautiful, Jared?" she asked, turning in the saddle to face him. She waved her arm toward the mountain range before them. "Wouldn't you give anything to just stay here and never leave?"

"It's tempting," he replied, watching her with a close eye. He was determined that when she appeared to show signs of tiring, they would head back to the house.

Their rides continued for the next few days. The evenings were spent quietly either talking or, a few times, Jared would put records on and they would dance before the large fireplace in the living room. Those evenings were the best, as far as Alex was concerned. She had come to enjoy those times Jared would take her into his arms even if it was only for the all too short moments when the music played.

As expected, Alex grew impatient to talk to Dena and find out what was going on, but Jared was adamant. No business phone calls until he said so. The one time she did sneak in a call to Dena, she was given the same set of instructions. She was just to relax and build up her strength.

"You've been living on nervous energy for a long time, Alex," Dena told her. "I'm just glad your illness wasn't more serious. Now, don't worry about anything here. Take advantage of everything," she chuckled. "Live it up, Alex. You're out in the wilds with one of the country's sexiest men. I'm sure you can take it from there." Still laughing, she hung up.

"Sure," she muttered when she left the study.

"Caught you!" A pair of arms snaked around her waist.

Out of reflex, Alex's hands snapped down to break the grip.

"Hey!" Jared yelled, grabbing hold of his pained wrist.

"I'm sorry," she apologized, turning around. "Old habits die hard, I guess."

"Remind me never to wake you out of a sound sleep," he muttered. "Is this what happens when a guy asks you out?"

Her head snapped up. "What?"

"Forget it. I don't think I want to take out a woman who could deck me if I decided to get fresh," Jared told her, pretending to turn and walk away.

"Jared." Alex reached out and lightly gripped his arm. When he looked down at her, she suddenly felt very shy. "Are—are you asking me out?"

"I had thought about it," he said off-handedly. "Nothing fancy—dinner and a movie, if you feel up to it."

Her smile lit up her face. "I feel up to it."

"Fine, then we'll leave here about six. And dress warmly," he said sternly.

Alex found herself looking forward to the evening and was glad there were only a few hours to fill before six. In dressing, she decided a pair of black cords and off-white bulky knit sweater would keep her warm enough under her heavy jacket. Jared had dressed casually in brown cord jeans and a gold-colored shirt.

They ate dinner in Santa Barbara in a popular restaurant depicting the 1920s. After careful selection, a movie was decided on.

Sitting in the darkened theater, Alex hadn't reckoned on a touching love story that would reach the depths of her soul. The tale of two lovers separated by fate and later joined brought tears to her eyes. A hand reached out and gripped hers tightly while a handkerchief was pressed into her other hand.

"It's allowed, you know." Jared leaned over to whisper in her ear.

"It's only a story." Alex sniffed. "It's not real."

"No, but it could be," he murmured, lifting her fingers to his lips. For the remainder of the film he kept Alex's fingers laced through his, lying in his lap or pressed against his mouth. She shifted uneasily in her seat, vainly fighting the heat in her blood from his touch.

When the film was over they slowly walked out of the theater still under its spell. Jared kept an arm draped over Alex's shoulders as they walked down the street toward the parking garage where the jeep had been left. At one dark corner Jared suddenly veered to one side and pulled Alex after him.

"What—?" Her question was abruptly silenced by the insistent pressure of Jared's mouth.

"I've been wanting this all evening," he said, sliding his tongue over the parted softness of her lips. "Hell, I've been wanting this ever since that night before you got sick." He angled his body sharply against hers until they were molded together.

"I'm not sick now," Alex breathed, running her palms over the hard muscles of his back.

"No," he groaned, plundering her mouth with his tongue, tempting her, seducing her with all his experience. His hands moved under her sweater to seek the warm skin of her midriff and upward. Inhaling sharply, he pulled away. "This isn't the place," he muttered roughly. "Damn! It's over an hour back to the ranch and I don't know if I can wait that long."

Alex couldn't speak, still entranced by the overwhelming spell Jared had woven about them. At that moment she wouldn't have cared where he made love to her as long as she assuaged the growing ache in her body. "We should go before we collect an audience," she murmured, pulling her sweater down over her hips.

Jared chuckled. "In a few minutes." He dropped a light kiss on her nose. "No use in letting the world know how I feel about you." He cocked his eyebrows at her and grinned crookedly.

Alex had to grin back. "You enjoy trying to shock me, don't you?" she accused him playfully.

"Trouble is, old salts don't shock easily," Jared said mournfully, putting his arm around her waist. "Let's go home. I have plans to take up where we left off," he added meaningfully.

Alex shivered at the sensual undertone in Jared's words. She knew that once they reached the ranch there would be no turning back, and she knew she wouldn't want to.

They walked along the sidewalk, their steps now faster because they had a purpose to their journey.

"Hello, Alex."

She spun around to face a man not much taller than herself and a pregnant woman standing beside him.

"Dennis, what a surprise." She greeted her ex-husband in an even voice. "Hello, Laura, how are you feeling?"

"Eagerly waiting for the day when I won't look like a circus elephant." The bright glow in her eyes cut through Alex's heart.

A set of fingers against her spine reminded her of her manners. "Dennis, Laura, Jared Templeton. Mr. Templeton, Dennis Page and his wife, Laura." The expression in her eyes gave him the rest of the story.

"Very pleased to meet you, sir." The younger man extended his hand. "I see your name in the business section of the newspaper all the time."

"Are you still stationed in San Francisco?" Alex spoke up, all the time wishing to terminate this conversation as quickly as possible and get away.

Dennis nodded, his eyes never leaving his wife. "We thought we'd come down for the weekend. Probably our last quiet one for a long time." His voice was warm and loving, indicating no regret.

"Dennis!" Laura reproved.

"I guess we should get back to the hotel. Laura doesn't like to admit she tires easily. It was a pleasure meeting you, Mr. Templeton." He turned to Alex. "It was good seeing you again, Alex." Her answering smile was tight-lipped.

The two couples parted, but not before Alex saw Dennis put a protective arm around Laura.

A grim expression crossed Jared's face as he took Alex's arm in a bruising hold and practically dragged her down the street.

"Let me go!" Alex ordered between clenched teeth. "Let me go!" She raised her voice.

Swearing under his breath, Jared pushed her down a narrow alley between two buildings.

"Where's my cold-blooded Alex now?" he demanded, boxing her in against the wall and leaning over her like an avenging devil.

"What do you mean?" Her eyes were narrowed in anger.

"My God, your tongue was hanging out while you talked to them! You envy your ex-husband's wife," he accused her.

"No!" She pushed against his chest for freedom, but he refused to move.

Jared's hand twisted painfully in her hair and pulled her head back. "Maybe he didn't recognize that hungry look in your eyes, Alex, but I did," he jeered softly. "You're jealous that Laura is carrying the child you could have had. You ache to create a new life." His other hand slid with insolent ease over the concave stomach and upward to find its way beneath the thin fabric of silk and lace. "You feel threatened as a woman. In fact, you feel less than one because you didn't carry his child, don't you?"

"Damn you!" she sobbed, raising one hand to strike him.

With lightning speed Jared's hand had left her breast to grasp the offending palm before it hit him. Grasping her wrist, he twisted it up behind her back, forcing her body against him.

"You've lost control, Alex," he taunted, his lips a breath away from hers. "It's only at times like this that I can believe you're a flesh and blood woman instead of a statue."

"You wouldn't know a flesh and blood woman," she spat at him, her eyes shooting sparks of green fire. "You've only had hollow shells, fakes just like you."

"Fake, am I?" he snarled. "You, of all people, should know better."

His hand in her hair twisted farther until she thought her neck would snap. Then something else had her attention. Jared's lips cruelly fastened on hers without any regard for the inner softness. He intended to prove to her who was in charge of this embrace. She was powerless to resist the searing heat of his mouth or even the hard length molded intimately against her. His tongue roughly assaulted her mouth while his hand released its grip on her hair and moved down to slide under her sweater, tearing open the front of her bra in order to reach her already swollen breasts.

A low moan rippled through Alex's throat, although no one could be sure if it was pain from Jared's harsh caresses or pleasure due to the small flames licking along her heightened nerve endings.

"Let go of my hand," she whispered against his lips.

Jared released her, knowing she wouldn't move away

from him now. His other hand feathered over her waist, down over her hips, then back to press against her buttocks and up against him. Alex's hands reached for the buttons of his shirt feverishly, needing to touch his heated skin. The grinding of his hips against hers expressed his need for her.

"I should take you here and now," he muttered hoarsely. His narrowed eyes took in her swollen lips with satisfaction. Her ragged breathing was no harsher than his own. At that moment he wanted nothing more than to leave his brand on her. He wanted the world to know she was his.

"I wouldn't let you," she lied, her breath still coming out in jerky gasps.

Jared's cruel smile cut her to the bone as his thumb and forefinger circled her nipple, making her tremble.

"It surprises me how much passion is under that cool exterior, Alex. You hide behind a mask, and I intend to find out what's underneath it."

"Don't be so sure of yourself." She lifted her chin, still refusing to give in.

Jared expelled a harsh breath as he realized their spot wasn't as private as he'd like it to be. "I never lose, Alex. I suggest you remember that," he stated matter-of-factly, pulling her sweater down over the waistband of her jeans and grabbing hold of her hand.

The ride back to the ranch was accomplished in tense silence. Their reason for a speedy return was now forgotten after the sight of Dennis and his wife. Alex stared out the window lost in thoughts of the past, thoughts that could only recreate pain.

When they reached the house, she hurried inside as soon as Jared unlocked the door.

"In a hurry, aren't you?" he jeered softly.

She looked up at him with narrowed cat's eyes. "Your

seduction plan failed, Mr. Templeton," she informed him in a cold voice. "Sleep well." She headed for her room and firmly closed the door behind her.

Alex felt very weary as she undressed and slipped on a ruffled nightshirt. She knew it wasn't the unexpected meeting with Dennis that upset her. She hadn't loved him the way she now loved—she gasped in horror at this new turn her thoughts were taking.

"No!" she moaned out loud, collapsing on the bed. It couldn't be that she was falling in love with Jared. Love was a foreign word in her vocabulary. It was the memory that she had pushed to the back of her mind and kept there that upset her. Switching off the light and curling up under the covers, she now couldn't keep back her tears—tears that streamed down her cheeks and dampened her pillow.

Alex was so lost in her self-misery she wasn't aware when the other side of her bed gave way and a pair of arms slid around her.

"Shh." Jared's croon was soft in her ear when he turned her to him and cradled her against his bare chest. "Go ahead and cry. Get it out of your system."

"Wha-what are you doing here?" she demanded between sniffs.

Jared rested his chin on top of her head. "This isn't the night to be alone," he murmured. "The best cure for you is a warm body to take away the hurt." He spoke slowly, as if the words pained him. "I can understand that it upset you to see your ex-husband again and that he appears happy, but you've done well for yourself too. Don't let your love for him tear you up, Alex. You have to give him up and live your own life."

She shook her head. "You don't understand," she sobbed. "I don't love Dennis anymore, if I ever did."

"Then it *was* the fact that his wife's pregnant." He

absently stroked her bare arm and settled her more comfortably against him.

Alex reached up, burying her damp face against his neck. "Not for the reasons you think," she sniffed. "You see, Laura is giving Dennis the child I lost."

Jared's body stiffened at her softly spoken statement. "What child, Alex?" His voice sounded constricted.

She breathed in the comforting scent of clean male skin and the spicy aroma of his soap along with the tang of the cheroots he smoked. Ironically, his presence consoled her.

"I met Dennis not long after I graduated from Annapolis," she began tentatively. "He's good friends with two of my brothers, a career man, and not my father's idea of husband material. He claimed Dennis was too soft and I saw him as the exact opposite of my father and promptly married him. I didn't love Dennis, not the way a woman should love a man, but I think, deep down, he didn't love me either. We were the blending of two illustrious naval families, nothing more. I still felt we could have a good marriage, but it didn't take long to realize that Dennis wasn't going to assert himself as a man."

"You once said he's a good man, too good for you," Jared quietly interjected.

Alex nodded. "Dennis didn't believe in raising his voice or arguing, while I grew up in a family who believed you had to shout to be heard. Arguing, to them, was as natural as breathing. Sometimes, in a fit of temper, I would accuse him of being less than a man," she sighed deeply. "Oddly, just when things looked their worst, I found out I was pregnant." Jared's arms around her tightened their hold. "I saw this as some kind of second chance, that we just might be able to make a go of it." The tears were now sounding in her voice and Jared's hand stroked her back to let her know he was there. "I decided to tell Dennis that evening but before I could tell him he had news of his own.

It appeared he had met someone a few months before and found something with her he hadn't had with me—love. Dennis felt that he wasn't truly hurting me because our marriage had been over for a long time. He loved Laura and wanted to marry her." She drew a deep breath.

"And the baby?" he prompted softly.

"I—er—" She stopped, her voice choked with tears. "I just couldn't tell him then. I made some idiotic excuse and left the house. Dennis was right; I didn't love him, but I also had the baby to consider. I went for a drive and decided to let Dennis have custody of the baby after it was born. A child needs two loving parents. It was then a drunk driver hit my car broadside and I lost the baby." Her voice was a mere whisper. "I told Dennis to go ahead and file for divorce and once I recovered, I resigned my commission. I was tired of my friends' pitying glances and the gossip behind my back. Poor Dennis was blamed for leaving me for another woman and I was blamed for forcing him into another woman's arms. There was no even ground when it came to the gossip. My father's tirade over my daring to divorce a navy man wasn't too pleasant either," she ended on a dry note.

"And then you ended up with another tyrant," Jared commented wryly.

Alex shook her head, keeping her body still burrowed close to him. "You're one only part of the time," she told him.

"I'm flattered." He shifted until he was lying against the pillows with Alex curled up next to him. "That's the most you've ever told me about yourself."

"You wouldn't have known if we hadn't run into Dennis and Laura tonight," she confessed, unconsciously sliding her silky leg over his bare hair-rough ones.

Jared's lips skimmed across her temple. "I was right, Alex. You do have guts." There was admiration in his voice. "You've been able to make an entirely new life for yourself without any bitterness showing. That says a lot."

She couldn't remember ever feeling as comfortable as she did then. She idly finger-combed the crisp, curling hair on Jared's chest. She was so relaxed, she wasn't even aware that her actions were having a noticeable effect on him.

"Hey." His voice came out thick as his fingers closed over hers to halt her sensual occupation. "No fair."

A slow smile tipped the corners of her lips. "What's no fair?" she asked huskily, the tip of her tongue tasting the salt of his skin.

"You know very well what," he muttered, carefully pushing her away.

In the darkness Alex's face was only a pale shadow. "There was a time this evening when you wouldn't have minded."

Jared's hands lifted to cup her face in an almost painful hold. "Don't act the tease, Alex," he said roughly. "So far I've been able to control myself pretty well, but you won't be able to push me much further."

She turned her face so that her lips and teeth grazed his palm. "Maybe I don't want you to control yourself," she murmured in a seductive purr.

That was all he needed to hear. Groaning, he pulled her back to him and covered her mouth in a fierce kiss of desperation. His hands slid under her body and positioned her over him until their shapes complemented each other.

"God, Alex, why do you do this to me?" Jared said hoarsely against the soft skin of her throat.

"Don't talk," she breathed, moving her hips suggestively against him. "Oh, please, Jared, for once in your life don't talk."

It wasn't long before Alex's nightshirt and Jared's briefs

were pushed down to the end of the bed and their naked bodies entwined among the covers.

Her fingertips teased the taut muscles of his stomach and beyond, learning what pleased him and guided by his groans while his own hands sought out her areas of pleasure.

"Alex." Jared's breath was hot against her parted lips. "Woman, you tie me up in knots." His tongue fenced intimately with hers in preparation of the ritual their bodies would follow. His mouth lowered to the sensitive cord on her throat, along the silky skin of her breasts, and down over the smooth plane of her stomach. The gentle rough tip of his tongue teased her navel, flicking in and out.

Alex gasped out loud as Jared's lips continued their sensuous journey. She was bursting into flames. When he moved up and over her, she received him eagerly, greedy to have all of him. Nothing mattered except the soaring flight he was taking her on. The slow climb, the plunging descent, then another, almost painful, climb to greater heights culminated in a fall into weightlessness. All she could hear was the sounds of Jared's harsh breathing and feel his body tighten, then expend his strength, and Alex's accepted and returned his gift. Afterward they were too exhausted to do more than wrap the sheet over their damp bodies and curl around each other to sleep.

Early the next morning, Alex was awakened by warm kisses planted along her neck and throat. Jared had pulled her back against his body and now tightened his hold on her.

"Um, good morning," she murmured, her voice husky with sleep.

"Thank you." There was a humble note in his voice. Something she hadn't heard before.

Alex twisted her head around to gaze at him with quizzical eyes. "For what?"

Jared's eyes were bright grass-green pools of color. She thought he was trying to tell her something, but the message eluded her.

"For last night," he said simply while his hands began their magical stroking again. "For trusting me enough to confide in me. Always trust me, Alex. Don't ever hide anything from me." By then his urgency had been transmitted to her. She turned in his embrace and, moaning softly, gave herself up to the rocketing sensations he created.

For the next week Jared was never far from Alex's side. During the day they explored the countryside either by jeep or on horseback. The nights were spent dancing to soft music or snuggling in Jared's bed, watching the flames dance in the fireplace and talking about anything and everything. During that informative time they learned more about each other than they had the six months working together. They were lovers, but most of all, they were friends.

That Sunday evening Jared pulled her into the bedroom and produced a bottle of wine for them to enjoy by the fire. He wore only a pair of jeans and was barefoot while she had put on one of his shirts in lieu of a robe after her shower. They reclined on the carpet in front of the fireplace, talking about their past dreams.

"Since I was a boy, I always had a desire to be a doctor," Jared murmured, his wicked smile reflected in his eyes.

"Are you sure you don't mean *play* doctor?" Her slow smile indicated she had caught the hidden meaning.

"Same thing," he agreed blandly, leaning over in her direction. The palm of his hand smoothed the collar of his shirt away from her shoulder. "I even memorized the

Latin term for every part of the body." He leaned over more and gently forced her back against the carpet.

Her arms lazily circled his neck. "How fascinating," she purred. "Tell me more."

Jared's lips traced a moist path along the lines of her throat and his words were provocative while his hands began their intimate wanderings. For every pulsing area he chose, he whispered the medical term, which made his examination all the more tantalizing.

Alex could feel a tightening within her body from Jared's palms grazing the tips of her breasts, then gliding down to cup the undersides before they moved downward to caress her stomach. It was only as his fingers trailed over her thigh and found sensitized spots that her gasps were impossible to hold back. She was in an agony that was more pleasure than pain. She reached out to the waistband of his jeans, unsnapped and unzipped them, but Jared held back with a teasing smile. Alex's eyes glowed in the firelight. By using every part of her body and the magic her fingers and lips wrought, he couldn't hold back from her long. Their fierce union was blessed by the orange firelight. There was more than cries and groans of pleasure; there was a blending of their souls when Jared's thrusting rhythm took Alex further than she had ever gone before. She held on to his body, crying out, not fearing the descent because she knew he would be with her.

Later that night, after a playful shower, and now bundled up in bed, Jared lay back against the pillows and pulled Alex down on his chest. He lit a cheroot and drew deeply.

"We'll be leaving for L.A. at nine," he announced quietly.

Her body inwardly tensed, although nothing in her demeanor gave her away. Inside her head she was screaming a protest at returning to civilization. She didn't want to return to the designation of Alex Page, Jared Templeton's bodyguard, but if she was to survive, she would have to do just that. Step back into that tiny square that made up her life.

Jared spoke her name softly, but she squeezed her eyes shut, pretending to be asleep. In reality, it was a long time before her mind cleared enough to drift off.

CHAPTER SEVEN

Alex stared out her office window experiencing the same restless feeling she had been suffering from for the past week.

There had been no flying visits to Jared's other offices, no press conferences where she was required to attend. Instead, she remained in her office catching up on paperwork and preparing a revised budget for her department while Jared paid a visit to Rashid's home in the tiny country of Kamar. Alex had not been invited to accompany him. She had been called to Jared's office the day he left and was informed that he was flying to see Rashid about some finalization of the contracts.

"How long will we be there?" she had asked him, uncomfortable with the way he seemed to avoid her gaze.

"You won't be going, Alex," Jared told her gruffly.

"I see." She didn't, or, perhaps, she did all too clearly.

This time he did look at her. "I'm traveling to a Middle Eastern country where women aren't viewed in the same light they are here. There could be problems for you that even Rashid couldn't handle. He has promised me full protection during my stay."

Alex managed a faint smile. "I guess I can get caught up with my work then." She turned to leave feeling very empty.

"Alex." She halted and turned around. Jared frowned with concern, or was it annoyance, that she wasn't more upset over being left behind? "Your movements would be sharply curtailed there," he went on to explain. "It wouldn't be fair to you."

"You're right, I would have problems over there. Have a good flight, and give Rashid my regards." She walked out of the office. An hour later Jared was gone.

In the past week Alex had heard nothing from Jared, while inside she prayed for a word, anything to let her know he still remembered her. The only word she received was from Chris through Jared's secretary Sara. They were due back that day, but she'd be be damned if she'd be there to give Jared a welcome home.

Alex had been surprised when Walt St. Clair came into her office the day before to apologize for his callous remarks during their last meeting. He admitted he hadn't been willing to listen to her recommendations and, as a result, they almost suffered a great tragedy. She was gracious in accepting his apology, although she had a suspicion that Jared had been behind Walt's visit. A chauvinist like Walt wouldn't do this on his own.

"Will you stop fidgeting?"

Alex whirled her chair around and faced Dena with a murmured "Sorry," but the expression in her eyes belied her words.

"Where's that domineering, no-nonsense boss who left here six weeks ago?" Dena demanded, laying some papers on Alex's desk. "She was much easier to handle."

Alex shrugged, appearing indifferent on the outside

while a bundle of nerves inside. Why was she so jumpy? "Culture shock after being out in the sticks for so long," she hedged.

Her secretary eyed her skeptically. "I might believe that from Chris, but not you." She studied Alex's set features for a moment, opened her mouth to say something, then closed it again. "Mr. Templeton is back in the swing of things even after that trip to the Mideast," she finally told her.

Alex didn't reply. Mr. Templeton had been in the swing of things from the moment he had boarded the company jet that Monday morning almost two weeks ago. She could still remember breakfast had been quiet, almost restrained between them.

When they had boarded the jet, Jared settled Alex in a seat, brought her coffee, and asked politely if she needed anything else. After receiving her negative reply, he had left her alone and immersed himself in a pile of paperwork and numerous telephone calls. Jared the lover was gone, and Mr. Templeton, the living force behind Fernwood Enterprises, had returned. Those idyllic days at Pradera Alta might never have happened for all the attention he gave her.

When they had landed at Los Angeles International Airport, a quiet Jared drove Alex home and assisted her upstairs with her luggage. When he turned to leave her, he briefly placed his hands on her shoulders.

"Don't rush into the office first thing." His quiet words were a huge disappointment to her. "You're still recovering and the work will still be there."

"I didn't get all that much rest," she couldn't resist retorting.

A muscle twitched in the corner of Jared's mouth. With a murmured "Take care" he left her.

Alex spent the remainder of the day unpacking and

putting away her clothes. By concentrating on mundane chores, she was able to keep her mind a blank and not recall the reason her body was so relaxed.

She now thrust those memories from her mind. In a matter of days she had reverted back to her old habits except for a few changes.

Alex joined a health club near her apartment and now used their facilities instead of the ones at the office. She never stayed late but instead took her work home and did it there, refusing to answer her phone if it rang or answer the doorbell the few times it pealed. She also lost the few pounds she had gained at the ranch and a few more besides that.

Dena's face shadowed with concern. "Alex, are you sure you're all right?" Her question wasn't out of curiosity, but affection for her boss. "Nothing's wrong, is it?"

Alex flashed her a reassuring smile, but the sparkle wasn't reflected in her eyes. "I'm fine, Dena, it's just getting used to the nine-to-five routine again, that's all."

Dena clearly didn't believe her manufactured reply, but knew better than to contradict her in the mood she had been in lately. Sighing, she left the office to return to her work.

When Alex left that evening, she wasn't surprised to see Jared's silver Maserati absent from his parking slot. He hadn't been keeping late hours either. At least not at the office. She hated to admit that the thought of him with another woman was enough to turn her stomach.

Alex was puzzled to find an envelope tucked under her windshield wiper. Then she knew. She didn't have to open it to identify the correspondent. Her fingers were shaking when she extracted the envelope and pulled out the folded sheet of paper. "Nico's tomorrow at 11:30" was written in a familiar bold slash. There was no signature, but there didn't have to be.

"No, thanks," she grated, crumpling the piece of paper in her hand. Why this after two weeks of silence?

A clear-eyed, more determined Alex entered her office the next morning. It took only one look for Dena to see her boss was plotting someone's demise and in the very far reaches of her mind she had a pretty good idea who that someone was.

Alex handled the budget meeting with the accounting department heads with that same determination, then returned to her office at eleven fifteen.

"Get your purse," she ordered crisply.

"What?" Dena looked up, then at the small clock on her desk. "What's wrong?"

"Nothing." Alex's smile resembled a very dangerous feline. "I have a wallet filled with charge cards that I intend using and I'd adore some company. We're taking a long lunch today."

"Yes, ma'am!" Dena snapped to attention. "Who am I to argue with the boss?"

Alex knew she was deliberately ignoring Jared's summons for lunch, but wasn't exactly sure why. She wanted to make sure he understood that she wouldn't jump when he snapped his fingers. There were plenty of women in this state alone who'd jump through his hoops, but she wasn't one of them and this was her way of letting him know that.

Alex and Dena toured as many boutiques as they could cram in for the next three hours and had the packages to prove it. Alex grimly thought of the many charge receipts in her purse and the whopping bills she'd receive next month. She only hoped she'd like her purchases just as much when she unwrapped them at home. Impulse buying had never been one of her habits. She hoped she hadn't set a precedent.

"Whew!" Dena let out a tired gust of air while they

entered the elevator. "I think you bought enough clothes to last you for the next five years."

"Good, because it will probably take me that long to pay off the bills," Alex joked.

When they reached the office, Dena checked in with the message center while Alex walked into her office and slipped her leather pumps off one pair of very sore feet. The shoes were comfortable for anything but all the walking she just did. She turned when Dena appeared in the doorway.

"Mr. Templeton's office has been calling every half hour since noon," the secretary announced. "I just now talked with Chris and he said to remind you of your three o'clock meeting with Mr. Templeton. A meeting you forgot to tell me about, therefore, it wasn't on your calendar," she scolded.

Alex hadn't forgotten to tell Dena because there had been no meeting planned for this afternoon. At least there hadn't been until Jared had arrogantly manufactured one and she knew why. She had ignored his lunch invitation and now he would demand to know why.

"Chris also said to tell you that Mr. Templeton's in a really foul mood," she warned. "He's already torn Chris's head off, so be careful."

Alex offered Chris a silent apology for bearing the brunt of Jared's displeasure with her. "I think I'll be safe enough." She heaved a weary sigh as she slipped her shoes back on. "I guess it wouldn't do to go up there in my stocking feet."

Sara greeted Alex with a wry smile. "It's not too safe in there," she advised.

"So I've heard."

Chris glanced out of his office and shuddered theatrically. "You're braver than I am," he told Alex in a rueful voice.

"We'll see," she murmured, then raised her voice. "Don't bother to announce me. I don't want you in the line of fire." She approached Jared's office door, turned the ornate knob, and entered without knocking.

Jared's back was to her while he gazed out the window. "It's about time," he grated.

"Shouldn't you identify your visitor before railing at them?" Alex asked lightly. An inner voice told her Jared's temper was at the boiling point, but she didn't feel the need to worry.

"I knew it was you." Now he turned around. "Where the hell have you been?" he demanded.

Alex was shocked by the new carved planes on Jared's face. If she didn't know better she'd swear he had been suffering from the same inner torment that plagued her. She mentally braced herself before she replied. "I had shopping to do."

Jared's movements were jerky as he lit a cheroot and drew deeply on it, then blew out the smoke. "I expected you at Nico's," he said finally. In a sarcastic voice he added, "Was your shopping so important you couldn't bother to let me know?"

"There wasn't an R.S.V.P. on your note." Alex's voice emitted a chill to the air.

He took several deep breaths but they did nothing to calm his temper. It was so frustrating to stand there and yell at her while all the time he wanted her back in his arms. He wanted to hear that cat's purr while he made love to her, to hear those throaty moans when he explored every inch of her satiny skin. He wanted to taste her mouth and see if it was what he remembered. Damn it, he *wanted* her!

"It shouldn't be this way, Alex." His voice hinted at the nights they shared.

Icy eyes sliced through him. "*What* shouldn't be this

way, *Mr.* Templeton?" She deliberately ignored his sensual undertones. She had no intention of giving in to him now. "You were the one who called this meeting. If there's nothing pertaining to Fernwood to discuss, I have a great deal of work to do."

A strange light flashed in Jared's eyes and a predatory smile curved his lips. "Are you that wary of me, Alex?" he asked softly.

"Yes." She saw no reason to lie. If Jared wanted to know, he could find out easily enough. She was only too knowledgeable of his methods. "But don't start patting yourself on the back yet, Jared. Because I am wary, I will take more caution around you. Thank you for this two-week breathing space." She paused, determined that this last thrust would find its mark. "And thank you for that extra week's vacation at your ranch. It was very instructive." With that, she turned on her heel and walked out, but not before she saw the white slashes in the corners of Jared's mouth. Her words hit a nerve with deadly accuracy.

Alex spent the rest of the afternoon in her office waiting for Jared to storm in and announce to the world that she was fired. When the clock showed one minute after five, she picked up her briefcase and for the first time in two weeks didn't take any paperwork home.

Alex didn't go straight home. She had too much energy boiling inside. She stopped at her health club and worked out, hoping to erase her inner frustrations. Instead, her unease only increased.

She spent the balance of the evening putting away her new wardrobe, all the time wondering if some of her purchases were wise.

For some unknown reason she chose a new nightgown to wear that night. She smiled to herself as she recalled

Dena's reaction to the bright red silk and lace nightgown that fell to the floor in body-hugging folds. A nightgown meant to be admired by a man.

Alex's restless thoughts continued as she tossed and turned in her bed. She had barely slipped into a light doze when the doorbell rudely interrupted her sleep.

She groaned a wish that the intruder would go away, and pulled her pillow over her head. Five minutes later, with the shrill buzz of the doorbell still penetrating her cocoon, she decided she would be better off to find out the identity of her visitor. Alex stumbled out of bed and pulled on a matching hip-length quilted kimono-style jacket.

"All right, all right," she muttered as she approached the door. She squinted through the peephole but the last person she expected to see was Jared, now dressed casually in jeans and a sweater. She barely remembered opening the door. "Jared! Is something wrong?" She scanned his shadowed features.

Without saying a word he hauled her into his arms. "Not now," he muttered, sliding an arm under her legs and lifting her up to cradle her against his chest. "Not now." He walked into the darkened bedroom and set her down on her feet. His hands lifted to slip her jacket off then slid under the narrow straps of her nightgown. It fell to the carpet, leaving her standing naked in a pool of red silk. Jared sucked in a sharp breath as slivers of moonlight filtered between the partially drawn drapes and highlighted her skin.

He kept his eyes on her as he hurriedly shed his clothes and steered her toward the bed.

Alex had kept silent because she truly didn't know what to say. She was startled to see Jared and even his presence, here in her bedroom, couldn't penetrate her numb brain. She could only stare up at his sharply etched features and pray she wasn't dreaming. She reached out to touch him with hesitant fingertips after he stretched out beside her.

"Jared, why are you here?" she finally whispered while her fingertips blazed a trail along the slightly bearded jaw.

He brushed his palms over her breasts, then suddenly slid his hands around to her back and drew her up to him. "I couldn't sleep without you." His words were muffled in her hair.

It wasn't the kind of admission Alex wished to hear. She braced her hands against his chest and pushed him away.

"How touching," she drawled icily. "Tell me something, Mr. Templeton, how did you manage without me for the past two weeks? Did it take you this long to go through your current list of bed partners?"

Jared's face first paled then reddened in anger from her attack. Before Alex could react, he had shackled her wrists with one hand and pulled them over her head while he trapped her lower body under his leg.

"You always have to get your digs in, don't you, Alex?" he ground out. "If anyone has suffered from your verbal nails, it's me and I've got the scars to prove it. No more, lady, I'm just not going to put up with it." All the while his hand roamed intimately over her body, touching and teasing those sensitive areas, delicately probing with sensual expertise. He was seducing her with his touch and it wasn't long before he could see Alex's reaction—the heavier breathing, her eyes bright with desire, the pupils dilated, the coral tips of her breasts blooming in silent invitation for his caress, and a lethargic heaviness to her limbs which were warm to the touch. Nor could she hold back the unconscious writhing of her hips arching toward him and seeking his potent desire. Alex could no more renounce her physical response to Jared than he could to her.

"It will only tear us apart in the end," Alex cried out, still denying the powerful force running through her body. "We'll be destroyed."

"Will we?" One large hand cupped her nape in order to massage the tension away. "We can't be destroyed, Alex. Don't you know that?" Jared's tongue snaked a burning path up her throat and along her jaw to her earlobe. There his teeth settled gently on the fleshy skin and pulled. "We're invincible together."

No, we're not, she thought to herself with eyes squeezed shut, forcing herself to reject the molten lava flowing in her veins. There's too much against us. Her thoughts weren't spoken out loud because, knowing Jared, she knew he would only brush her fears away. Fear. What a strange word for her to use. Alex hadn't known fear one day of her life except . . . no, she mustn't think about that! She gasped when Jared's mouth had worked its way down to her breast.

"We're two of a kind, Alex," he murmured. "Cold on the outside, but underneath is enough dynamite to blow up the whole damn state." His hand wandered over her flat stomach, then lower until he found her warmth. Alex's hips arched against the teasing fingers seeking that high plane that only he could take her to.

She was powerless to argue any further. Moaning softly, she wrapped her arms around his neck and nestled her fingers in his hair. The tension in her body was growing with each moment and by the time Jared's body lowered to claim hers, she was ready to scream out her frustration. His thrusting body soon brought her higher than he ever had before, and she could only snuggle up to him so that she wouldn't be alone in this glittering netherworld. Jared grunted softly when Alex's teeth sank into his shoulder but not once did he slow or halt the rhythm that brought them close to fulfillment. When it came, Alex could only cry out Jared's name and cling to him with a merciless grip. A moment later he shuddered and gasped out her name.

She wasn't sure how much later it was when she slowly returned to reality. Jared's damp body was curved tightly around hers and she could detect his breathing returning to normal.

Alex thought back to those moments when nothing mattered but her cravings for Jared's body. That's all it could be—physical desire. Even in the beginning she had tamped down any stirrings she had for him, knowing nothing could come from it. And now? Could they share more than just passionate moments in bed? Could they share love? Because now she was only too aware that she had committed the ultimate crime of falling in love with her boss.

No! The word screamed through her mind. *Don't do this to yourself!*

Her sudden tension had communicated itself to a drowsy Jared.

"Alex, what's wrong?" he asked while rubbing her back with a comforting hand.

"Nothing," she lied, glad the darkness hid this still new knowledge from him. She was beginning to wonder if she hadn't been fighting these feelings all along.

Jared fell into a deep sleep, keeping a possessive arm over her waist, but it was a long time before Alex drifted off into a troubled slumber.

A scant few hours later Alex was vaguely aware of a comforting warmth leaving her. She slowly opened one eye and saw Jared dressed and tucking his shirt into his jeans. Turning, he noticed her and walked over to squat down next to the bed and drop a swift hard kiss on her lips.

She could taste the minty flavor of her toothpaste on his mouth.

"Sorry I woke you," he whispered, brushing the stray strands of hair from her face.

"What time is it?" She found it hard to focus her eyes.

"A little after four." Jared grinned at Alex's painful groan. "I have to drive home and change my clothes before going into the office. Do me a favor, don't stand me up for lunch today."

"I won't eat any breakfast so I can order a large meal," she promised, yawning deeply.

His fingers curled lightly around her neck. "A few pounds here and there wouldn't hurt. Go back to sleep, love. I'll come by your office at eleven thirty."

The last thing Alex remembered before she drifted back to sleep was her blankets being tucked firmly around her shoulders so that she wouldn't get cold. Then she was left alone to sleep and dream beautiful thoughts.

After that night Alex and Jared's relationship took another turn. Even though she now knew she loved him and realized he held at least some affection for her, she still was very careful around him at the office.

Although Jared now spent an average of three to four nights at her apartment and they lunched together at least once a week, she refused to acknowledge the fact that many would view her as his mistress.

When Jared had to fly to Chicago, Alex may have been given a separate room, but she didn't sleep alone. There may have been a snowstorm outside, but inside she slept in the warmth of Jared's arms. On the flight back to Los Angeles, Chris eyed them curiously but wisely kept his thoughts to himself.

Alex's demeanor softened and even her wardrobe reflected her new self. The clothes she had bought on her impulsive shopping spree showed less severe lines, although the jackets were still cut a little fuller to accommodate her shoulder holster when she wore it.

The days passed and Alex could only watch and wait to see where time would bring her in regard to Jared's life. She feared the day when he would no longer want her, but she wasn't about to sit and wait for the worst to happen. She would enjoy today and not worry about tomorrow.

CHAPTER EIGHT

One Friday evening Jared came by to take Alex out for dinner.

"What exciting destination do you have in mind, Mr. Templeton?" she asked lightly, knowing her ice-blue lightweight wool dress would suit any occasion.

"You'll find out soon enough," he merely replied in a mysterious voice.

Out of unconscious habit, Alex walked over to her small desk in the living room, unlocked the top drawer, and reached in for her gun. Seeing her intent, Jared swiftly crossed the room and placed his hand over hers to stop her.

"You're not on duty tonight, Alex," he said quietly. "This stays home."

She looked up at him, surprised by the intensity in his low voice. She didn't like carrying it any more than he liked her having it on her person, but those letters threatening Jared's life were still fresh in her mind.

"I may not have a black belt in karate, but I would do what I could to defend you," he said with a faint hint of self-mockery in his voice. He took her hand out of the drawer and closed and locked it.

"I never doubted it, Jared," she said honestly.

He smiled wryly. "I do. You forget I saw that mugger you took care of."

Dinner was at a small exclusive seafood restaurant in Beverly Hills, where the clientele was insured privacy. Alex and Jared had dined there several times before knowing they could have a quiet dinner and not be bothered by any aspiring members of the press. Since Jared's business dealings with Rashid had been publicized, he had been given little private time of his own. After dinner they drove to a nearby club for dancing.

Alex hated to admit she felt self-conscious when she went out with Jared, although there was no reason for her to. All the time she had grown up she had socialized with many young men and women on the same social level as Jared, if not higher. Naval and diplomats' children all shared one thing in common; they had to grow up fast in order to survive the rigors of life in Washington D.C. Yet this was different. She could compete with him on a social level when it came to background, but she still considered herself a working woman even if her profession wasn't the normal nine-to-five job.

It was all right when they were alone in her apartment or even when they met for lunch, but dinner was a more intimate meal to her way of thinking. She was fearing the day when he'd realize he was making the grave error of sleeping with an employee and abruptly stop their affair. She hated the word, but what else could she call it? She couldn't deny how much it would hurt. She had seen it happen to Jared's mistresses in the past, so why wouldn't it eventually happen to her?

When Jared's arms slipped around her while they danced, she felt secure. She had been feeling extremely tired lately and it seemed as if the evening was already catching up with her.

"Tired of my company already?" Jared teased lightly, catching her trying to stifle a yawn.

"I'm sorry," Alex apologized. "I don't understand it, we went to bed early last night." She turned red as she realized the implication of her words.

He chuckled in her ear, all the time enjoying her discomfort. "Tell me about it. I got a good-night kiss and you were out like a light. Talk about feeling rejected," he teased.

She laughed softly at his woebegone expression. "Poor baby," she mocked affectionately. "I guess I'll just have to make it up to you, won't I?" Her fingers were buried in the soft hair at his nape and gently rubbed the slightly rough skin. It didn't take long to see a reaction. To reinforce her dance-floor seduction, Alex's body moved in perfect time to Jared's, making sure to brush against every vital part. Her face nuzzled his throat and the tip of her tongue snaked out to steal a taste of his salty skin.

It wasn't very long before Jared took her hint. He guided her off the dance floor and over to their table, where he picked up her purse and coat. "Let's go." There was no mistaking the message in his husky voice.

Although Jared drove out of the parking lot, he steered the Maserati in a different direction from the freeway that led to Alex's apartment.

"Are you kidnapping me, sir?" Alex asked throatily, snuggling up to him and teasingly placing her hand on his thigh.

"Sure am."

"Hmm, will there be a demand for ransom?" She bent her head and playfully nipped at his throat while her hand wandered up his thigh.

"No." His voice was thicker now. "Damn it, Alex, if you keep that up, I'm not going to be able to drive!"

She gurgled with laughter. "We could always check into a motel," she suggested, her fingertips drawing lazy circles along his inner thigh. "At this rate that could be an excellent idea, not to mention a real time-saver."

"Not with what I have in mind," he rasped. "Now try to keep your hands to yourself for a little while longer."

"Five minutes?"

"Twenty."

"Fifteen," she compromised.

"Twenty," he repeated. "And that's with pushing the speed limit."

Alex laughed; the wine from dinner and the brandy she had consumed at the club had released her inhibitions. "I can see it now," she declared theatrically. "But, officer, I couldn't help it, this crazy woman had her hand in my lap!" She continued laughing. "Hmm, wouldn't that look good on your record, although I don't think it's exactly against the law."

"It's called creating a public nuisance," Jared told her.

"Your five minutes are up," Alex announced, holding her arm up to look at her watch.

"Good, then you only have fifteen more minutes to wait."

By then she was filled with curiosity as to their secret destination since Jared wouldn't give her any hints.

The car traversed the quiet streets of Brentwood until it slowed in front of a pair of stately wrought iron gates. Jared depressed a switch under the dashboard and the gates slowly swung open.

As the car moved along the winding driveway, Alex knew where they were. The tightening of her stomach muscles told her.

"This is your house," she said unnecessarily.

"Give the lady a cigar." Jared stopped the car in front of the house and switched off the engine. He half-turned in the seat. "Care for the fifty-cent tour?" he asked quietly.

Alex nodded. In the darkness all she could make out was the outline of a two-story Tudor-style house. Right away, she could sense the lack of warmth and comfort the ranch house radiated.

"What, no butler?" she asked flippantly when Jared unlocked the front door.

"Staff's night off," he explained.

"Naturally," she murmured, stepping inside.

The interior was spacious and attractively furnished, obviously by a decorator's hand, but it still lacked warmth. Jared took her into a small drawing room and poured two brandies.

"It's a lovely house," Alex volunteered, feeling the need to say something.

Jared's lips quirked with a wry smile. "A little overpowering?"

"A lot overpowering."

There was a brief, companionable silence while they each sipped their drinks.

"Care to see the rest of the house?" he asked in an all too casual voice.

There was the faintest hint of a smile on her lips. "I thought you'd never ask."

Jared reached over and took the balloon glass out of her hand and set it on a nearby table. His hands circled her wrists and pulled her to her feet.

"Now that you've seen the downstairs—" He drew her out into the hallway and toward a curved stairway.

"I've only seen your hallway and drawing room," she reminded him, looking around and seeing several other closed doors.

"There's really nothing else interesting down here. Upstairs is the important room." His husky voice danced along her skin.

"Oh? And what can that be?" Alex asked, throwing her arms around his neck.

Jared bent slightly and scooped her up in his arms. "The master bedroom," he answered, biting her earlobe. "What else?"

She laughed, burying her face in his neck. "Hmm, I like this method of transportation," she purred. "It's very romantic."

Jared's idea of showing her the master bedroom was to toss her onto the large bed and lean over to pull off her clothes. Alex wasn't going to argue. She merely reached up and helped him off with his. She remembered little of the room except that the bed was large, the mattress firm, and Jared's warmth surrounding her. That was all that mattered when she later fell into a deep sleep with Jared's arm thrown possessively over her waist.

In the early morning hours Jared was suddenly awakened by the thrashing body beside him. Levering himself up on one elbow, he surveyed Alex's restless figure and the sound of her whimpering cries ripped through his heart. He began to take her in his arms when her pained words momentarily stopped him.

"No, please," she begged in a little girl's voice. "It's dark and there's nasty things out there. No, Daddy, please don't make me stay there!" she screamed.

Jared then scooped her into his arms and gently shook her awake. "Alex, baby, it's all right," he crooned. "It's only a nightmare. Shh. I'm here, no one's going to hurt you, I swear it." His hand smoothed the tangled hair from her damp face. "It's okay, baby."

Alex's eyes flew open, but they looked at him blankly. "Jared?" she croaked, clutching him tightly. "Please, don't let him make me stay there. Please." She snuggled up against him, rubbing her body sensuously against his. With her lips and hands she aroused him to the point of no return and loved him to fever pitch. While Alex had been the aggressor in their lovemaking before, it had never been with the intensity of tonight, as if by loving him she would exorcise the horrors of her dream.

Afterward a stunned Jared lay back with Alex now sleeping peacefully in his arms. The last time he had awakened her from a nightmare, which sounded suspiciously the same as this one, she had rejected his comfort. Tonight she had made wild love to him as if to keep the shadows away. His mouth tightened as he recalled the words spoken before he had awakened her. Tomorrow he would demand to know the truth and she would tell him whether she wanted to or not.

The next morning, when Alex awakened, she found Jared standing over her with a large tray in his hands.

"Breakfast, my lady," he announced formally, handing her one of his shirts to use as a robe.

"Hmm, I could get to like this." She smiled up at him as she accepted the shirt and slipped her arms through the sleeves.

Jared sat on the edge of the bed and picked up the second coffee cup. "You had another nightmare last night," he remarked in a deceptively casual voice.

Alex flushed and ducked her head. "I'm sorry if I disturbed you," she muttered, refusing to look up at him.

Gentle fingers cupped her chin and tipped it upward. "Alex, what did your father do that was so terrible it's haunted you all these years?" he asked tenderly.

Her features turned to stone. "I don't know what you mean," she lied.

"Yes, you do. Last night, after I awakened you, you made love to me as if you were afraid it would be your last time. The surprising part was that there was almost a violence to your lovemaking, as if you were trying to get back at all men for something that had happened years ago," he added dryly. "Now I know what it means to be used and abused."

Tears filled her eyes. She pushed the tray away, not even wanting that as a barrier between them. Alex flung her arms around him and buried her face against his throat. "Oh, Jared, I've never been really afraid of anything but my nightmare," she whispered.

"Tell me about it," he coaxed, smoothing her hair back with his hand. "Get it out in the open and I swear it will never bother you again."

Alex was hesitant to dredge up old memories, but she knew Jared was right. The only reason it kept coming back to haunt her was because she refused to admit its existence except in her sleep.

In slow, halting words, she told him about the disadvantages of having four brothers and a father determined that she would do as well as her brothers in everything they did, if not better. Her naval career was to be as outstanding as all the Haydens'.

That included the test of maturity at the age of ten held at the family home in Louisiana where they were expected to spend the night in the nearby forest. With each word Jared's hold tightened with anger at the unfeeling father who forced his daughter to do something against her will. A child who had been unable to stand up to the man and refuse to participate in the test. Her father's theory had been if her brothers could do it, so could she.

She told him how she was afraid to leave the forest in the middle of the night and likewise terrified to stay. A ten-year-old child's imagination is unlimited and any animal, real and imagined, seemed to visit the young Alex. After that she ended up with nightmares that had haunted her throughout her adult life.

"Not anymore," Jared said grimly. "I'll make sure they'll never come back." It was the closest he had ever come to a commitment.

Alex's arms loosened about his neck while her tongue traced lazy patterns on his throat. "So you felt used and abused, did you?" she murmured.

"Sure did." A teasing note entered his voice. "We'll have to leave here in the next twenty minutes or so in order to have enough time to get you home to change if we plan to drive down to San Diego for lunch."

"Twenty minutes!" She gave an unladylike snort. "If you think this is going to be a morning quickie, buster, you've got another thing coming!" Her hands had already strayed to his belt.

He grinned wickedly as he momentarily stopped her busy hands. "Just as long as we get there in time for dinner."

"Deal."

Alex was having another of her bad days. It was more than a headache; her entire body ached and she felt ready to explode.

This Wednesday had been spent looking for a file that had been in its rightful place if she had only looked there first.

"Why didn't you tell me that?" she demanded shrilly of a surprised Dena who had never seen her boss lose her temper over such a small matter. In fact Alex usually laughed and said how grateful she was to have a secretary who filed correctly even if the boss couldn't understand an ordinary filing system. Looking at the concern in Dena's face, Alex only crumpled and dropped into her chair, the tears beginning to fall. She covered her face with her hands, moaning her wish that she'd quit crying.

"Alex . . . Alex!" Dena was instantly at her side. "What's wrong?"

"Oh, who knows," she sniffed, accepting the tissue offered to her. "I seem to be doing this quite a bit lately."

"No harm in that." The secretary laughed. "I was real good at that when I was pregnant with Roddy. For some strange reason tears and pregnancy go very well together. Hormones or something."

Listening to Dena's careless words, Alex grew very still. She raised paper-white features, then reached for her desk calendar and flipped back through the pages. The calculations in her head weren't very reassuring.

"Alex?" Dena sounded concerned.

"Would you please call Dr. Garrison's office and see if there's any chance of getting an appointment this afternoon," she requested in a low voice.

Recognizing the man's name as Alex's gynecologist told Dena enough. "Certainly," she murmured.

Alex was given a two o'clock appointment and she decided to take a long lunch. The fact that Jared hadn't tried to contact her since she left his office hadn't given her very much peace of mind and she needed to have some time to herself before she went to the doctor's office.

Dena was in Alex's office laying some memos on her desk when she returned.

"What's the old saying?" she asked wryly. "Something about the rabbit dying?"

"It's Mr. Templeton, isn't it?"

Alex nodded, knowing it wouldn't go any further than those walls. She felt very tired and the strain was showing on her face. She kicked off her shoes and dropped into her chair.

"Are you going to tell him?" Dena asked her.

Alex shook her head with an emphatic toss. "No!"

"This may sound out of line, but aren't you on the pill?" Dena asked quietly.

Alex smiled wanly. "Oh, yes, I'm on the pill but a lot of good that did. When I had that rash, the doctor had prescribed prednisone and warned me that it could inhibit the effectiveness of the pill. Naturally, you find it hard to believe that it can really happen until you're the one on the receiving end. Jared didn't take precautions since he knew that I was." She took a deep shuddering breath.

"I always wondered when the explosion would happen between the two of you," Dena mused.

Alex glanced up. "What?"

The secretary laughed. "There's been some kind of current flowing between the two of you from the very beginning. I don't think anyone else noticed it. At least I never heard any gossip about it. I could sense it though. I just figured it would be a matter of time before detonation."

Then another thought occurred to Dena. "You're not considering an abortion, are you?"

"No!" Alex was horrified at the idea. "No, I'll tell Jared, but not just yet." She sighed wearily. "Do me a favor and hold any calls for a while."

Dena nodded, understanding Alex's need for privacy just now and left her alone.

Alex sat back in her chair. She found it hard to imagine another life was growing inside of her body—a life she and Jared had created. One thought caused her to smile. The child would definitely have green eyes.

According to her calculations the baby would have been conceived the night she had told Jared about her marriage. The night he had made such tender, all-consuming love to her. It seemed only right that a child would result from such a night.

She wasn't sure what she was going to do. She just knew that she would take better care of herself from now on. At least she now knew what was causing her queasy stomach during the past few weeks and could stop blaming it on drinking too much coffee.

Alex wasn't surprised when Jared showed up at her apartment that evening even though she hadn't heard from him all afternoon.

"Okay, I want the whole story," he greeted her with a growl.

"What story?" she asked, puzzled and a little wary of the wicked glint in his eye.

"Chris referred to Veronica Sayres as the infamous Chicago Cannonball when he talked to Sara. Is this another one of your private jokes?" he demanded, once again feeling jealous of the strong friendship between her and his assistant. He had come up from behind and slid his arms around her waist to pull her back against him. "Talk, lady."

Alex began to laugh. "I wondered when you'd finally hear about that. Come on, you have to admit the name fits," she said waspishly.

"True," he agreed readily. "May I ask what game this is?"

"Same as Chris and I placing bets," she explained. "We always gave your current mistress a suitable nickname."

Jared seemed to flinch at the word *mistress,* making her wonder if that was how he saw her.

"Merrilee Tanner?"

"The Houston Handful."

Jared grinned, understanding the meaning of the name all too easily. "Gina Valenti?"

"Venice Vampire."

"Marina Delgado?"

"Madrid Menace."

"Lauren Wellesley?"

"Boston Bombshell."

By then Jared was laughing at Alex's clipped replies. "No one can touch you for ingenuity, love." He grinned. "Come on, let's go out for dinner."

Alex couldn't understand why she felt heavy-eyed during dinner until she remembered the doctor telling her she might grow sleepy for no reason at times.

"I'm sorry," she mumbled her apology when they had returned to the apartment and Jared took charge of undressing her and putting her to bed. After tucking her in, he discarded his own clothes and climbed in beside her.

"For what?" He drew her back against him. "We had that flight to Seattle a couple of days ago and the one to St. Louis before that. It's just jet lag."

"Yes, but we haven't—I mean you—" She couldn't find the words.

"Alex," he chuckled in her ear. "Don't you know that I don't stay here just to ravish your sexy body. If I did, I would just put you to bed and leave. I'm here because I enjoy just being with you."

"Oh, Jared." She turned over and burrowed her face in his chest. "You're too nice for your own good sometimes, do you know that?" She yawned deeply.

"Go to sleep, love," he soothed, rubbing her back in a comforting manner.

The last Alex remembered was Jared's low voice lulling her to sleep.

The following morning she wasn't so lucky when she had her first real bout of morning sickness. She felt as if the nausea had turned her stomach inside out. It didn't help when an alarmed Jared followed her into the bathroom, washed her face afterward, and carried her back into the bedroom.

"I don't know what's wrong," she lied, offering him a weak smile. "Maybe something didn't agree with me from dinner last night."

"And maybe it's a relapse," he replied, carefully tucking the covers around her. "I'll fix you a cup of tea."

Alex smiled at the thought of Jared puttering in the kitchen. "Are you sure you can?"

He looked affronted at her idea of his being totally helpless with such an easy task. "I think I can manage it."

"Could I have a few crackers too? They're in the cabinet by the refrigerator."

Jared smiled down at her. "Anything you want. I'll be right back."

He left later after ordering Alex to stay in bed for the rest of the day. She waited until her doctor's office opened, called, and received a prescription for medicine to relieve the nausea. Since her stomach still rolled a bit, Alex took it easy for the rest of the day and kept in touch with Dena by phone.

"Now all the symptoms begin," the secretary warned her with a soft laugh. "Morning sickness, backaches, strange food cravings in the middle of the night. How well I remember it all."

"Terrific." Alex groaned, adding sarcastically, "Thank you so much for your concern, Dena. I really appreciate it."

The secretary's voice sobered. "I gather you haven't told him yet."

"Not yet," she hedged.

Alex usually didn't enjoy playing invalid. She certainly hadn't at the ranch. Now she discovered it was nice to have someone fuss over her. She was touched by Jared's frequent phone calls to her, asking how she was feeling and making sure she was staying in bed.

That evening he fixed her a light dinner and kept her entertained with stories about his day. Alex thought wistfully how much like a married couple they sounded. She also wondered what Jared's reaction to the baby would be and several times thought of bringing up the subject but lost her nerve. If he hadn't married by age forty for the sake of having an heir, would he want one now?

She felt pleased that he talked over his problems with her, but it bothered her that he was making their relationship known in the office in subtle ways.

"Jared, you may be the boss, but please look at my side," she told him. "I won't be accused of securing my position through your bedroom."

His face hardened to granite while the expression in his eyes spelled doom to anyone who would dare malign her.

"Has something been said to you?" he demanded.

Alex shook her head. A faint smile twisted her lips. "Would *you* take on someone who could break your arm as easily as if she were filing her nails?"

Jared grinned. "No way, lady. Of course, as you said, I'm the boss. My clout just happens to be a little different from yours."

"It must be rough at the top," Alex mocked.

He grinned devilishly. "Depends on what I'm on top of . . . or whom."

The next afternoon when Jared had a luncheon meeting, Alex called Chris.

"I'm in the mood for a thick, gooey pizza," she announced. "I even have Dena talked into going out for it. Want to come down for an Italian orgy?"

"No contest." He laughed. "In fact, bring it up here and we'll use the conference room."

While they ate the thick slices dripping with cheese and a variety of toppings, Chris eyed Alex sharply.

"It seems we don't share as many of these impromptu lunches as we used to," he commented casually.

Alex showed no sign of reaction on the outside, although she knew exactly what Chris was getting at.

"Probably because you gave up betting with me," she said lightly.

"Or because Mr. Templeton has found himself a Los Angeles Lady," he countered with a strange edge in his voice.

Alex took a sip of her wine and slowly set her glass down. She looked up and studied him.

"I've always considered you a friend, Chris," she said quietly. "If you have something to say, say it and don't go about it in a roundabout way."

He fixed her with a steady gaze. "I don't want to see you hurt, Alex. You're a lovely lady, you're fun and intelligent. You know that. I don't think you're the type to go along in life as one of Jared Templeton's discards."

"Well," Alex murmured, feeling the pizza sitting heavy in her stomach. "You certainly don't pull any punches, do you?"

"You're an adult and hopefully know what you're doing. I just felt the need to speak up," Chris explained.

Alex leaned forward and cupped her palm around his cheek. "I understand," she said softly. "Thanks, friend."

"I hope I'm not interrupting something." Jared's cold voice fell on them.

Chris jumped back, looking guilty even though nothing had happened. Alex was slower to turn in Jared's direction. Every action was deliberate and she'd be damned if she'd allow him to make her feel guilty!

"Mr. Templeton." She smiled, totally at ease, her arms draped over the sides of her chair. "Was your meeting a success?"

Jared's gaze was cutting her to bits. "For someone who's such a workaholic, you certainly know how to take full advantage of your off hours," he sneered, then turned on Chris. "There's a stack of notes on your desk that need to be compiled. I expect it done by the end of the day."

"Yes, sir." Chris hastily jumped to his feet and left the conference room. He sensed a storm brewing and he didn't care to be around when all hell broke loose.

Alex remained seated, watching Jared through narrowed eyes. "And what are my orders for the day?" Her soft voice was coated with steel.

Jared glanced around at the pizza carton and glasses of wine. He walked over to the table, picked up Alex's glass, and finished the contents. "Very cozy," he ground out.

"If you hadn't been tied up with those bankers from London, you would have been invited."

"Sorry, I don't like being a third wheel," he gritted out.

"And what do you like?" She knew she was courting trouble by egging him on when he was in this mood.

He slammed the glass down. "What else do you two share besides lunch?" he demanded.

"Watch it, Templeton!" Her low voice spelled her silent plot for his demise. "Don't say something you'll regret because then I'll say something I just might not regret."

"Damn it, Alex, he's in love with you!" Jared rasped, white lines of tension visible around his mouth.

She jumped to her feet. "I know it. I also know he's a very good friend," she informed him.

"And what am I?" he demanded.

That was the last question Alex expected to hear. She briefly closed her eyes, then looked straight at him. What was he to her? She only wished she could give him the right answer. She drew a deep, shuddering breath.

"I don't know, but at times like this, I wish I had never met you." She brushed past him and started to leave the conference room, then spun around. "I'm sure there won't be anything wrong if I take the rest of the day off. After all, it is one of the benefits of being the boss's mistress, isn't it?" Ignoring Jared's harsh command to return, she hurried out and down to her office.

Alex grabbed her briefcase, told a startled Dena she was going home, then left. She knew the last thing she needed just then was another confrontation with Jared. Her churning stomach was warning enough.

When she reached her apartment the telephone was ringing. She waited until it stopped, picked it up, and laid the receiver aside.

Alex was surprised that Jared didn't come by that evening. For the rest of the week he stayed away from her and she had no word from him until Chris called to say they'd be flying to Denver the following Monday.

On Monday morning, for the first time in weeks, it was Frank who picked up Alex instead of Jared. She felt as if another part of her life was ending and she had no idea how to stop it.

Alex sat back in her seat wishing the faint queasiness would go away. How could she have forgotten her nausea pills today?

"Here's your tea." Chris leaned down and handed her a steaming cup. His good-natured grin was replaced by a concerned frown. "Are you sure you're all right, Alex? You look pale."

"I'm fine," she assured him with a wan smile. "It's probably just a touch of the flu."

After Chris left her, she leaned her head back and closed her eyes. She was going to have to tell Jared soon. She was already beginning to round out a bit and her skirts were taking on a snug fit.

A few moments later her nervous system told her she was under observation. Opening her eyes, she saw Jared staring at her across the jet's interior.

Even with the short distance separating them, she could feel the electric current flowing in a direct line to her. Nothing had to be said. Jared's eyes hotly caressed the contours of her face, moved down to her lips, and seared the soft skin of her throat. Alex's stomach tightened at the blatant heat in his gaze. There was no mistaking the silent message. Jared was recalling their nights together and decided he wasn't going to let her go—yet.

This new, softer Alex felt the desire to cry. She wanted more than his body; she wanted his mind and his love.

She dozed a little, not awakening until the jet was ready to touch down.

"The press is waiting," Chris informed Jared while they prepared to disembark.

Jared clearly wasn't happy at the idea. "I wonder who tipped them off when we'd be returning," he snapped.

"Somebody who wants to give you an ulcer." Alex slipped her jacket on. She felt very tired and was looking forward to going home and going to bed. She was hoping Jared wouldn't decide to make his reconciliation with her tonight. She was afraid his sharp eyes would detect her physical changes and question her. She didn't care to discuss the baby with him just now.

The hatch opened and the stairs were lowered. As she descended the jet, Alex could detect the uneasy prickles along her nape. She didn't like this feeling. Her eyes roamed over the waiting crowd and along the edges of the group. There was something very wrong here. Everything may look all right, but her sensitive antennae were telling her different. Once off the jet, she walked at Jared's side and a little ahead. She wasn't going to take any chances.

"Give us the scoop, Mr. Templeton," someone called out in an unfriendly voice. "What's the truth behind you buying Sheikh Kalim's oil wells? Why all the secrecy?"

Jared cursed explicitly under his breath.

"Come on, Mr. Templeton, out with it. Are you financing Sheikh Kalim's strategy to regain control of his country?" one belligerent voice rang out.

"Yeah, Mr. Templeton, how does it feel to be the treasurer to a dictator?"

The questions flew at Jared with the sharpness of many knives. Airport security guards had appeared to keep the group in order.

Alex had to admire Jared's calm replies. She knew it took every ounce of his self-control to keep hold of his temper under the barrage. She still felt uneasy and kept a constant surveillance of the crowd. Deep down, she knew a danger was present. She only hoped it wouldn't choose to show itself.

"When did you begin financially backing wars, Mr. Templeton?" another voice shouted.

Alex wasn't exactly sure why she turned her head when she did, only that the silvery flash caught her attention.

"Hold it!" Her voice rang out, stilling Jared's audience. In one fluid motion she had pulled her gun out of its holster, stepped in front of Jared, and pushed him to one side. Pure instinct told her where to aim and shoot even as an answering shot cracked. When the fire rammed into her body, she at first stiffened, then slowly crumpled to the ground with Jared catching her.

CHAPTER NINE

"Alex!" Jared groaned, cradling her limp body in his arms. He looked up, his features contorted in pain. "Damn it, someone call for an ambulance!" He gazed down at her waxen face and murmured over and over again. "Alex, darling, look at me," he pleaded. "You're going to be all right. I swear you will."

She slowly opened her eyes and looked at him through a pain-filled haze. Her body was burning up from the fire raging through her veins.

Her mind was screaming, *The baby! Please, Jared, don't let anything happen to our baby!* But her dry lips couldn't form the words. Her eyes pleaded with him, except he couldn't read her message. She closed her eyes against the blinding glare of photographers' flash bulbs and heard Jared's voice shouting at them.

"Get out of here, you bastards!" he roared, his face twisted with rage.

When the ambulance arrived, Jared was still reluctant to relinquish the now unconscious Alex and insisted on riding with her. During the harrowing ride he continually assured her she would be all right. Not once did he think her injury could be life-threatening.

The hospital emergency room staff thought nothing of a woman bleeding profusely in the shoulder from a gunshot wound being wheeled in on a gurney or even a man wearing a blood-stained suit running in behind.

A doctor ran up, examined her, and barked out a number. He spared a brief glance at Jared before he followed the gurney into an examination room. Five minutes later he walked out and over to Jared.

"Are you her husband?" the doctor asked him.

Jared shook his head. "Will she be all right?"

The doctor grimaced. "She needs immediate surgery. Is there a member of the family we can reach right away to sign a surgical consent form?"

"I have the power of attorney to sign any forms on Mrs. Page's behalf," he replied in a hoarse voice. "I want everything possible done for her. I'll pay whatever is needed in the way of specialized care."

For once someone wasn't impressed with Jared's importance. "Mr. Templeton, not even your money can buy what she needs right now. See the nurse over there, and she'll give you the proper forms."

Jared was standing at the counter filling out the forms when Chris rushed in.

"How is she?" he asked his boss.

"They're not sure," he replied dully. "She's going into surgery now." He looked down at the paper and muttered a fierce expletive under his breath. "Remember the day Alex started work? She insisted I have power of attorney to sign any medical forms in case of a situation just like this." He laughed harshly. "I laughed and assured her it would never happen. Never happen." His voice broke. "Hell, I don't even know when her birthday is."

"July thirteenth," Chris supplied quietly. Then he added, "You love her, don't you?"

Jared shut his eyes tightly, wishing the image of Alex falling to the ground and a stain of red spreading over the front of her light blue suit would disappear. He feared it would haunt him forever. "Love her?" he rasped. "She's my very breath. If anything happens to her, I'll—" He choked off.

"Alex is going to be fine," the younger man assured him. "Come on, let's get some coffee."

For the next few hours Jared remained in a tortured state of mind. Chris sat with him, offering silent comfort.

The nurses directed admiring eyes toward the handsome man with the pain-etched features and glazed eyes which continually watched the electronic doors leading to the operating rooms.

When a man dressed in sweat-stained surgical greens walked out, Chris saw him first and tapped Jared's arm. Jared jumped to his feet.

"Mr. Templeton?" The gray-haired man flashed him a weary smile. "I'm Dr. Matthews."

"How is she?" Jared demanded in a low voice.

He looked Jared's tired figure up and down. "I understand she took the bullet meant for you. Judging from where it entered her shoulder, I'd say it would have hit you in the heart."

Jared flinched, not at the thought of being shot himself, but at the idea of the pain Alex had gone through for him.

"She's going to have a very close eye on her, for tonight at least." The doctor smiled reassuringly at Jared's look of pain. "Oh, not only because of her wound. I'm calling in an obstetrician. I feel confident that the baby isn't harmed, but I'd still like an expert's opinion. If all is well, there shouldn't be any reason why she won't have a normal birth. I'm just taking some extra precautions until we know for sure the baby is all right."

Jared's face turned gray. "Baby?" His stiff lips could barely form the word.

Dr. Matthews nodded, his sharp eyes not missing his reaction. "Mrs. Page is about three months along. The fact that she's in such excellent health helped." He laid a hand on Jared's arm. "You're worn out, Mr. Templeton. Go see her, but I'll warn you she's so hazy from medication she won't know you."

"Go on," Chris urged gently. "I'll wait here."

A few moments later Jared quietly entered the Intensive Care Unit and a nurse led him to Alex's bedside. He inwardly groaned at her paper-white features and the monitors reading her vital signs and various tubes inserted in her body.

"Alex," he choked, touching her cool skin with shaky fingers. "Oh, love, why didn't you tell me?"

Ten minutes later the nurse ushered him out.

Chris watched a shadow of the true Jared approach him. He was shocked by the tears glistening on the other man's cheeks.

"Jared?" At that moment they were two men sharing a concern for a loved one.

"She's carrying my baby, Chris," he whispered, suddenly looking much older than his forty years. "She never told me. I guess I must have been too wrapped up in myself to notice the symptoms—the upset stomach and tiredness." He drew a shuddering breath. "She's pregnant, yet she thought nothing of risking her life for me."

Chris thought for a moment. "I wouldn't call that in the line of duty. I'd call it love." He touched Jared's shoulder. "Come on, I'll call a cab. You need to rest."

"Cancel all my appointments until further notice,"

Jared ordered. "I'll be staying here until she's out of danger. You also better contact her family."

"It's already been done. I didn't think they would want to hear about it on the eleven o'clock news. Alex's father is in Europe, but I left a message. Her mother is out of town also. Her one brother is going to try to get hold of her."

Jared came back to the hospital later that night and by using his undeniable charm was able to sit by Alex's bedside. She slept deeply, under the influence of the medication they gave her, unaware of her visitor.

Early the next morning, just after dawn, Alex finally stirred. Feeling a heavy cloud in her brain, she slowly opened her eyes and tried to focus them on the shadowy figure slumped in a nearby chair. She licked her dry lips trying to form words.

"Jared?" Her voice was barely audible, but he heard her.

The figure straightened up. "Alex!" He reached her bed. "Thank God!" Trembling fingers cupped her face.

She raised her arm and touched his cheek with curious fingertips. "You're crying," she said, her voice filled with awe.

Jared's face was haggard from his traumatic night but now creased in a warm smile filled with relief. "Happy tears, love," he assured her in a husky voice. "You've been having a nap. How do you feel?"

"Thirsty," Alex whispered, still in suspense over seeing Jared's eyes filled with tears. Why was he crying?

He reached back to pull the chair next to the bed and dropped into it. He leaned over and cupped her face between his palms. "You scared the hell out of me, lady." His voice held a ragged edge. "I hate to tell you how many gray hairs you gave me from all of this."

She carefully raised her free hand and lightly touched

the wings of gray at his temples. "You don't have to worry, they only make you look more distinguished." She smiled faintly, then asked, "Did I hit him?"

Jared drew a deep breath, wishing he could forget the events of the previous day. "You got him in the fleshy part of the thigh."

Alex wrinkled her nose. "I must be losing my touch. I had aimed higher," she said ruefully. "Was he part of that terrorist group that's been sending all those threats to you?"

He nodded. "I talked to Chris this morning right after he talked to the police. They're some outcasts from Rashid's country who don't want Americans buying their oil. They're all for keeping it back for as long as possible to drive the price up. They figured if they had gotten to me, the deal would have been called off and no one would be too eager to deal with Rashid for a while. They had planned to make their point all too clear with my death and a statement made to the press." He groaned seeing the look of fear on Alex's face at the thought of them killing him. "Oh, baby." There was so much he wanted to say, but where could he begin? He wanted to question her about their baby, about her reasons for shielding him with her body, risking her own life to save his. He wanted to tell her how much he loved her, but where did he begin when all he wanted to do was touch her, to reassure himself that she was real? Jared's hands lightly stroked the damp hair from Alex's forehead and cheeks and brushed the moisture from her eyes. He presented her with that special smile of his and leaned down to brush his lips over hers in the softest of kisses that was more stirring than any of the passionate embraces they had shared in the past.

"So you're awake." A nurse in her early twenties with the name Sheri printed on her badge greeted Alex with a cheerful smile. She was all business while shaking out and slipping a thermometer between Alex's lips and checking her pulse and blood pressure. She turned to Jared and presented him with a stern demeanor. "I believe we allowed you to stay in here only with your promise that you would notify us when she awoke," she scolded the unrepentant man.

"May I have some water?" Alex asked once the thermometer had been extracted and her vital signs recorded.

"Sure can." Sheri poured some water into a plastic glass and lifted her head to help her drink. She turned her head in Jared's direction. "You're being kicked out, Mr. Templeton." There was no nonsense in her bright voice.

Alex's eyes shifted in Jared's direction. She couldn't remember ever seeing such hunger in a man's eyes. Her first real thought was to ask about the baby, but she didn't want to in front of Jared. There just might be a slight chance he didn't know.

"I'd like to stay a little longer." He spoke quietly, without a trace of his usual self-assurance.

The nurse shook her head. "We've been breaking enough rules for you as it is. Out."

Jared walked back to the bed, leaned over, and dropped a light kiss on Alex's lips. "I'll see you later," he murmured.

"During visiting hours," Sheri reminded him.

Alex managed a weak smile at the nurse. "That's something new," she commented. "Mr. Templeton doesn't usually take orders so meekly."

"Well, he has from us if he wanted to stay in here with you. I sure have to tell you that you're the lucky one," Sheri chattered. "I wouldn't mind a sexy hunk like him hanging over me all night."

"I've been out since yesterday?" All Alex could remember was stepping in front of Jared and a shaft of fire hitting her body, then nothing. "My baby?"

Sheri smiled reassuringly. "Just fine. No problems there. We'll call Dr. Matthews to let him know you're awake, so he'll be in soon. Of course he's not as good-looking as Mr. Templeton, but he's a very nice man."

"Jared stayed here all night?" Alex found it hard to believe.

Sheri nodded. "We couldn't have gotten him out of here with a crane. Now, you just relax and I'll be back in a few minutes."

Alex lay back, lost in her thoughts. Jared stayed here all that time! The memory of the fierce hunger in his eyes just before he left haunted her until she fell asleep.

The next thing she remembered was a cool hand resting against her cheek. Funny, she never thought of Jared's hand being cool, it was always very warm on her skin or it seemed that way to her. She stirred, straining to find his heated body, but the movement only served to bring pain to her chest.

"Ooh!" she moaned.

"Careful or you'll ruin all my lovely needlework." That definitely wasn't Jared's voice.

Alex's eyes flew open. Now she remembered. She looked up at the gray-haired man smiling down on her.

"I'm Dr. Matthews, Mrs. Page." His quiet voice was soothing. "How are you feeling?"

"You tell me," she said feebly. "You're the doctor."

He chuckled. "Mr. Templeton told me the best way to know you're getting better is when you start making jokes. I think he's right."

"Dr. Matthews, are you—" She hesitated, afraid to voice her fears out loud. After all, there was no assurance that the nurse knew everything.

He patted her arm in a fatherly manner, instantly reading her thoughts. "My dear, your baby is just fine," he reassured her. "There's no reason why you won't have a normal delivery when the time comes."

Alex's eyes lowered to the tubes strapped to her arms. "When do I get rid of these?"

"If all goes well, tomorrow." His fingers pressed against her wrist while he checked her pulse. "An improvement over yesterday when you were first brought in, and much stronger than even a few hours ago. Now to get a look at my handiwork." He drew the sheet back and pulled her gown down to inspect the stitches. "Hmm, healing nicely."

The door opened and Jared stuck his head in. "Am I allowed to come in?" he asked.

Alex looked up and silently beseeched the doctor.

"Come in, Mr. Templeton." Dr. Matthews invited him in with a warm smile. "Mrs. Page is doing very well."

"I had no doubts." Jared entered the room carrying a large vase filled with yellow roses and feathery ferns.

"Oh, Jared!" Alex breathed, watching him place the vase on the bedside table. "They're beautiful."

"No more than you." Oblivious to their audience, he pressed a searing kiss on her lips.

"I think you just raised the lady's blood pressure." Dr. Matthews made some notations on Alex's chart. "I'll see you later, Mrs. Page."

"Alex, please."

"All right, Alex, I'll be in later. Don't hesitate to ring for the nurse if you feel any pain. Mr. Templeton." He nodded in Jared's direction, then left.

Jared took the chair he had sat in the night before and leaned over to cradle Alex's face between his palms.

She smiled up at him. "I'm glad to see you went home to get some rest," she said softly, reaching up to caress his freshly shaven cheek.

His hands tightened on her face. "Alex, do you realize

you could have been killed with that fool stunt," he said fiercely. "You and our baby could have died. God, what would I have done without you?" he demanded hoarsely. In those words, he told her who mattered most in his life.

Her eyes filled with tears. "I couldn't let him kill you, Jared," she cried softly. "And not because it's my job either."

"Oh, Alex," he groaned, resting his forehead on hers and rubbing gently. "Why didn't you tell me about the baby? You've known for quite a while, haven't you?" he accused her.

She nodded. "I didn't know how to tell you," she confessed.

He drew back slightly and looked as if he couldn't believe his ears. "One way is to just say, 'Jared, we're having a baby.' See how easy that is?"

"*I'm* the one having the baby," she argued, her old self already returning.

He smiled, not put out by her retort. "I had a hand in this too, you know," he informed her.

"She's *my* baby," Alex maintained stubbornly.

Jared smiled mysteriously as he rested his hand on her abdomen. "Let's just say you're keeping *him* safe right now."

Alex would have argued further, but a sudden movement sent waves of pain through her body.

Jared's face contorted as if he shared her pain. "Do you want something for the pain?"

She shook her head. "No," she said hoarsely. "I've taken up enough of your time lately and I do appreciate the flowers. You don't need to feel you have to come here. I know how busy you are."

"I wish you were well enough so I could practice a few judo throws on you," he said darkly. "Get this straight, Alex Page, I'm here because I want to be, not because I feel I have to. Don't you realize how much you mean to me?"

He would have said more, but a commotion outside stopped his words.

"I don't care who you are, young woman, I came to see my daughter and that's what I intend to do," a deep voice roared.

"Oh, damn," Alex groaned, closing her eyes. "Now I do feel sick."

The tall, lean, dark-haired man dressed in a naval admiral's uniform stalked into the room. A pair of dark green eyes very much like Alex's raked over Jared with merciless ease, then swung around to her.

"That was pretty stupid to get shot like that," he rasped, approaching the bed. "You look like hell."

"Jared, this is my father, Admiral Theodore Hayden," she said dryly. "Dad, Jared Templeton."

"So you're the one who got her shot." Even his normal voice resembled a bellow.

"No, I'm the one who would have stood in her way if I had known what was going to happen," Jared replied in an even voice, a danger sign in itself that his temper was beginning to boil.

Alex settled back. She had an idea this was going to be a show to enjoy.

Her father turned to her. "Your mother is on the verge of a nervous breakdown because of you. I told her she was better off staying in D.C. taking her tranquilizers than coming out here and having hysterics. I was in Switzerland attending a conference and I can tell you that this piece of news didn't help my concentration any."

"I'm sure Alex will more than compensate for her thoughtless behavior once she's on her feet." Jared's words were liberally coated with acid.

"It's going to hit the fan any moment now," Alex murmured to herself.

"Alex was better off in the navy!" the admiral roared. "At least there she wasn't getting shot at!"

"Except for that time at Pearl when I helped bust that drug ring," she spoke up. "The lead really flew then." All of a sudden she was feeling a great deal better.

"You be quiet!" her father ordered.

"Admiral Hayden, I suggest you remember this is a hospital and not a ship filled with midshipmen," Jared said icily. "If you can't treat my fiancée with the respect due her, then you better leave."

Admiral Hayden's eyes bulged and his face grew even redder while Alex looked just as stunned.

"Alex isn't the kind of woman who would be considered the ideal wife and mother," the admiral answered arrogantly.

Alex's eyes flew to Jared, silently pleading with him not to tell her father about the baby. Her stomach was already churning under the forces swirling between the two men. She figured a combination of her weakened state and her pregnancy was lending to her low mental energy.

"If you cared to know your daughter better, Admiral, you'd discover Alex has changed over the years," Jared stated coolly. "As this show of temper isn't helping her recovery any and I'm sure you're weary from your long flight, I'll put my car and driver at your disposal." He smoothly guided a still blustering naval admiral out of the room.

Alex could only lay there fighting the urge to laugh. She had never thought she'd be privileged to watch her father outwitted. She was still chuckling when Jared returned.

"Poor Frank." Her voice was filled with mirth.

"Are you sure he's not a spy for the marines?" He collapsed in a chair.

Alex now sobered. "Jared, I realize that my father may not be the warmest man in the world, but did you have to lie to him like that?"

A puzzled frown creased his forehead. "What lie?"

"About our being engaged."

"But we are, darling," he said matter-of-factly, then looked down at his watch. "Damn! I have a meeting with those London bankers in an hour." He stood up and walked over to the bed and leaned over to drop a hard kiss on her lips. "I'll be by this evening, love," he murmured, caressing her with his eyes. "Just be a good girl, do what the doctor says, and you'll be out in no time."

"We have to talk about this," she said desperately.

"Later." He silenced her protests with another kiss and left.

Alex didn't lack for visitors that afternoon between Chris and Dena stopping by for short periods of time. Her father had also returned, this time more subdued.

"Do you think marriage might work out for you this time?" he asked her.

"There's an element of risk in anything you do," she hedged, then was relieved to see Dena walk in and the conversation ended.

Jared hadn't come by the time visiting hours were over and Alex found herself missing him. She suddenly needed to see his solid form, to have some reassurance that he cared for her. Even if it wasn't love, she'd take what she could get just now. She knew only that she needed him.

The next morning the IV tubes were taken out and she was allowed a light breakfast.

"Got to keep Baby well fed," Sheri said cheerfully, placing the tray in front of Alex.

Alex eyed her meal suspiciously. "I hate poached eggs."

"Soft food is better for a stomach that hasn't seen food

in a while," she told her, then left her alone with her breakfast.

"Pregnant women need hearty meals, not baby food," Alex muttered to herself.

"I heartily agree."

She looked up at the sound of the familiar voice. "Jared!" She was so happy to see him she held her arms out in greeting. Once cradled in his arms, she pleaded, "Please, tell them this isn't enough. I'll starve here!"

"I think this is the last place that would let you starve." His shoulders shook with suppressed laughter as he looked down and surveyed her soft-boiled egg and cooked cereal. "That looks terrible!"

"Tell me about it." Alex wrinkled her nose.

Jared sat on the edge of the bed and kept hold of her hands. "I see you've been set free." He referred to the IV tubes.

"Do you think you could smuggle in a candy bar for me? Something caramel and lots of peanuts?" she begged.

"No," he whispered, leaning down to kiss her nose then farther down to her mouth. Just before it could deepen, he drew back. "I brought you something," he said casually, reaching into his jacket pocket and bringing out a small jeweler's box.

Alex froze, her eyes focused on the box even as Jared flipped it open to reveal a marquise emerald ring with a sparkling diamond on each side.

"I always felt diamonds were too cold for engagement rings," Jared said quietly. "I borrowed your opal ring for the size." He picked up her left hand, but before he could slide it on the appropriate finger, Alex jerked her hand away. He looked up, clearly not happy with her reaction. He waited for an explanation.

"No," she said hoarsely, shivering, but not from any chill. "I won't let you do this."

"You don't have any choice in the matter, Alex," he informed her in his steel-edged voice. "The wedding will take place just as soon as the doctor feels you're well enough."

"No!" There were tears glistening in her eyes. She didn't want another marriage that didn't have love on both sides.

"Yes!" Jared roared, jumping to his feet and pacing the floor. "Stop acting like a child, Alex. You've tried my patience long enough over this."

"You never had any patience!" she argued.

"Not when it comes to you!"

"I won't have you marry me just because of the baby." Her voice choked off on the last word. "You wouldn't have to worry that I'd deny you your child, but we can't get married just because of that."

Jared spun around. "Is that what you think? That I'm marrying you because of the baby?"

"Why else would you marry me?" Alex asked wearily. Arguing with Jared had become so tiring lately.

"Probably because I love you!"

The words may have been shouted at her, but the sincerity was there. Alex stared at him, praying she hadn't misunderstood him. "You love me?"

He walked back over to the bed and sat on the edge. Alex went willingly into his arms and burrowed her face in his neck, inhaling his masculine scent. His hands stroked her spine and moved up to wrap around her neck.

"Oh, Alex," he sighed. "You're stubborn, a bit of a shrew, and you could throw me across this room if you felt better, but for someone who has been in naval intelligence, you can be so dense at times. I've been attracted to you ever since you began working for me and I've been in love with you ever since the night you caught that mugger."

A wistful smile tugged at the corners of her mouth. "You fell in love with my physical prowess?" she teased.

He shook his head and lifted her hand to slide the ring on her finger, then raised it to his lips. Grinning, he nibbled on her fingertips. "I admit I've had my share of women over the years, but I finally realized I had nothing to show for my life. I wanted a wife and family and I wanted to lead a normal life." He smiled wryly. "Oh, I admit you were the last person I expected to fall in love with, but I didn't have a chance. It didn't take me long to know you were the only woman I wanted in my life." He slid his lips over each finger, bringing a familiar heat to Alex's body. "You were spitting fire at me that evening for putting Simpson in his place, and I decided then that I wanted you even if you yelled at me like that for the next fifty years." He shook his head in wonder. "Something tells me our marriage will not be quiet and uneventful."

"You never told me before that you love me," she murmured, caressing his lean cheek with her free hand. "And here I thought I was suffering from unrequited love."

Jared's eyes lit up. "Are you sure?" he asked huskily.

She grinned. "As sure as I'm pregnant."

His eyes darkened with remembered pain. "I swear, if you ever pull a stunt like last week again, I'll beat you," he rasped, pulling her into his arms. "It's been hell this past week, Alex; they couldn't reassure me that you'd recover completely. I even told the doctor to do anything to keep you safe, even if it meant taking the baby."

"I'm sorry I didn't tell you," she whispered, rubbing her cheek against his.

"I should have recognized the signs," he berated himself. "If I had known you were pregnant, you wouldn't have gone on that trip." His voice roughened with emotion. "I was afraid to leave you, Alex. I was so afraid that if I left here, you wouldn't wake up."

"Oh, Jared," she breathed, not bothering to brush away her tears.

His embrace was urgent yet mindful of her injury. "The media say I'm one of the most powerful men in the country, but not one cent of my money or any of my so-called power could take your pain away. I never felt so damn helpless!" he choked out.

Alex's new insight into Jared tore at her heart. Was the dampness on her face from her tears or his?

"I don't suppose you'll let me continue as your bodyguard," she mused thoughtfully.

He drew back. "Damn right I won't!"

"Then I demand the right to hire your next bodyguard. Someone who resembles King Kong will do nicely." She folded her arms in front of her.

"I have a much better idea," Jared said mysteriously, and no amount of coaxing from Alex could get the information from him.

"Mr. Templeton!"

They looked up to see a frowning Sheri standing in the doorway. "What are you trying to do?" she demanded.

"Have a heart." He grinned. "The lady just agreed to make an honest man out of me. I'm not going to be an unwed father after all."

"Jared!" Alex couldn't help but laugh. She decided she liked this lighter side of him much better.

He turned back to her and pressed his hand against her cheek. "You'll never regret it, Alex," he vowed quietly.

She turned her head to press her lips into his palm. "I know."

A month later Alex stood in the master bedroom at Pradera Alta and looked out the window at the surrounding darkness that didn't penetrate the firelit room.

Her burgundy silk and lace nightgown fell to the carpet in graceful folds, but did nothing to hide the slight rounding of her stomach. A scrolled gold band decorated her hand along with her emerald ring.

The wedding ceremony that afternoon was kept small and private. Jared had told her that the fewer the people the better. He also confessed that he was afraid a large wedding would scare her off!

Alex's mother had flown out from Washington, D.C., for the wedding along with her brothers and their families.

"If I didn't know any better, I'd accuse you of staging a shotgun wedding," Jared had teased Alex.

"Me? They're all too busy telling me what a great person you are," she teased back. "I think they'd disown me if I called it off now."

After a reception held in Jared's house in Brentwood, they flew up to the ranch for their honeymoon.

Alex turned when the door clicked open. Jared, dressed in a forest green velour thigh-length robe, walked in carrying a bottle of champagne and two glasses. He closed the door and leaned back.

"Hello, wife," he murmured, his voice heavy with sensual meaning.

"I'm nervous," she confessed, holding out a trembling hand. "Look at this, I can't stop shaking."

Jared chuckled. He set the bottle and glasses on a nearby table. "You? I'm the one who should be nervous. Marriage is new to me."

"Yes, I know, but I've never been married to you before," Alex said softly, gazing at him with love-filled eyes.

Jared uncorked the champagne, filled one glass, and partially filled the other. The latter was handed to Alex.

"That's all I get?"

He nodded. "And you're lucky to get that much. You're only getting it because it's a special occasion."

They touched glasses and sipped the bubbly wine. Alex

set her glass down and reached for Jared's glass to place it next to hers. She molded herself to his body and threw her arms around his neck.

"Did you know that a woman's sex drive increases during pregnancy?" She presented him with a bewitching smile.

Jared's mouth grazed across her lips. "No, but I'd be willing to do an intense study on the theory." His hand covered her swollen breasts and angled his fingers under the lace. Alex's response was a throaty purr of pleasure.

"Then why are we standing here making inane conversation?" Her fingertips teased the crisp hairs of his chest and strayed downward past the ties to his robe. Her smile widened when she found proof that Jared wasn't immune to her. "This experiment is performed much better in a horizontal position," she informed him softly.

"I think you could be right." Jared slid the nightgown straps down Alex's arms and pushed it the rest of the way down while she was occupied in untying his robe and sliding it off his shoulders. He bent slightly to pick her up in his arms, grunting, "Hmm, putting on a little weight, aren't you?" Then he yelped when Alex's teeth nipped his earlobe.

She was laid on the bed with tender care and he followed her down. "It's been a long time, Alex." His mouth moved moistly over her throat and down to the rounded curve of her breast. "Too long."

Her hands found his hair and tugged impatiently, urging him to find the darkened, taut nipple. "That wasn't my idea," she reminded him.

Jared looked up, a wry smile on his lips. "I wanted to wait until after the wedding." His wandering fingers circled the softly rounded mound of her stomach. "Are you sure it's safe?" he questioned anxiously, his concern now overshadowing desire. "We don't have to, you know."

Alex chuckled softly. She pushed at his chest and rolled him back. "Maybe *you* don't have to, but *I* certainly do," she informed him huskily.

He grasped her forearms and pulled her over him until they were warmly merged. His hands cupped her hips and coaxed her into the sensuous rhythm their thrusting bodies demanded. His voice hoarsely urged Alex on until her cries were followed closely by his own.

They lay in a warm tangle of arms and legs. Jared's hand slowly rubbed Alex's back, stopping occasionally to find a sensitive area.

"Hmm, two weeks of peace and quiet," she sighed. "I love it already."

"How about we keep it up on a regular basis for the next fifty years?" Jared asked matter-of-factly.

Alex lifted her head. "What?"

He lightly kissed her lips. "Meaning, I'm thinking of handing Fernwood over to the board and working there only on a part-time or consulting basis. I have an option on the Arabian stud farm not too far from here. Think you could handle coming up here on a fairly regular basis? Oh, we'd have to live in L.A. most of the time, but we'd definitely have more time to spend up here. That I promise you."

"Yes," she said without hesitation, then hugged him tightly. "Oh, Jared." Her voice bubbled with laughter. "I didn't want to tell you this, but now I feel I can. I hate your house in Brentwood."

"Love me, love my house," he said glibly.

"No, just you."

Jared's hand absently caressed her abdomen. "Think he'll enjoy coming up here as much as we do?"

"She," Alex corrected gently.

Jared smiled wryly. "You'll probably have all girls just to spite me."

"If I remember my basic biology correctly, it's the male who chooses the child's sex," she reminded him.

"Knowing you, you'll find a way to outwit basic biology."

Alex's hands were busy stroking Jared's chest and moving slowly downward to his heated desire. "Find a way how?" she asked seductively.

Jared's probing fingers returned the gesture. "I think you already did."

LOOK FOR NEXT MONTH'S
CANDLELIGHT ECSTASY ROMANCES ®